DRAGON'S TEMPTATION

RED PLANET DRAGONS OF TAJSS BOOK FIFTEEN

MIRANDA MARTIN

CONTENTS

ASHLEE

*W*alking into the lab my shoulders slump and my feet start to drag. I sigh and trudge my way over to my station, flopping heavily onto the raised stool. Pushing some slides around on the workstation, I try to push past the mind-numbing monotony.

It isn't that I hate the place, exactly. Being productive is good. I like the people, and some of the work is interesting. But every time I step inside the lab my chest tightens, my heart thumps, and the weight on my shoulders returns.

Starting the moment I open my eyes, the realization that today, like yesterday, and the day before, and the day before that I'll go to the lab hits me. It continues through breakfast —which I linger over as long as I can, trying to push away the inevitable moment.

My morning walk through the city seems longer each day as every step takes me closer to another day of doing the same damn thing I did the day before, with only the slightest changes. I thought science would be... exciting. The thrill of discovery, pushing on the boundaries of the unknown. In the old vids, on the ship, it was always thrilling. What I wouldn't give to have something exciting happen now!

It isn't hate. It's less intense than that... more a gradual wearing away of myself. All right, that sounds almost more depressing than hate.

"Good morning, Ashlee," Errol says without looking up from the workstation in front of him.

"Hey," I respond, shifting on my hard stool.

Maybe I should bring in a cushion, my butt is going numb already. Errol doesn't seem to mind the hard stools in there. There isn't the slightest sign of discomfort in the way he sits. Of course, with the Zmaj being so dragon-like and replete with tails and wings, I don't think he could sit in anything resembling a "normal" chair. Normal for a human anyway. Everything on Tajss is harsh, even the furniture.

"Ugh," I grunt.

Errol is the resident "mad dragon scientist" visiting from the Tribe once again. The Tribe is another group of Zmaj dragon-warriors that live in a cave system a ways off from the City. Fortunately the Zmaj have managed to get along, mostly, which goes against their natural instincts.

Errol is hard at work again, which is way more often than I would've expected considering he doesn't live here. Nothing can stop the guy. His dedication is downright impressive. He clearly doesn't have the mixed feelings I have coming in here. At least it doesn't seem like it.

Realizing I'm stalling—again—I tear my eyes from Errol and look at the piece of meteorite glass on the bench in front of me. This one's from the batch that was collected after the light show in the sky. Errol and Addison thought maybe the meteorites from after the colored streams of light in the sky might produce a different kind of glass when they hit the sand and melted it.

That prediction turned out to be true.

2

Problem is, there's still no clear indication pointing to exactly how we could utilize that difference. Nothing in the lab can measure its frequency, though one of the lights in the Invaders' ship had a reaction when Errol ran initial tests on the material.

Perfect.

Now all we need to do is ask one of those sweet Invaders who are always attacking our settlements what that changing light could mean. I'll get right on that. Staring at the sparkling glass, I try to fight sluggishness that settles on me every time I enter the lab. I'm bored. So, so bored. I want to throw things, stomp my feet, and yell until it all goes away. Like a two-year-old throwing a tantrum. Great, exactly how I want to be thought of.

"Ashlee?"

My name pulls me out of the black spiral of despair. Sarah is standing next to my station, smiling. Sarah was Rosalind's right-hand gal, before she hooked up with Drosdan. Now she lives with him over at the Tribe's Caves. What is she doing here?

"Yes?" I ask, standing with a frown. "Is something wrong?"

The hair on back of my neck stands on end and my stomach roils. It's got to be another attack by the Invaders; something's happened. Why else would she be here?

"No, nothing like that," she says, waving away my concerns. "Rosalind wants to speak with you, if you have time."

Oh. I don't even have to think about it.

"Sure, when?"

"Now, if you can," she says, looking around.

There's no stopping the smile on my face.

"Sure!" I say, failing to keep the enthusiasm out of my voice.

I've secretly been hoping I'll be posted somewhere—anywhere—else, for quite a while. Science was never anything I thought I would pursue with any kind of seriousness. It's fascinating, but I kind of ...fell into it when I got here. A basic understanding and mild aptitude were all it took for me to be assigned to work in the lab. Realistically, I would say my interest has always been more at a hobby level.

Actually practicing it... yeah, not really my jam.

It's damn near mind-numbing designing and running the same experiment over and over again with only minor tweaks between each iteration of it. Carefully noting each variable, each slightest change, all under Addison and Errol's watchful, ever-present eyes.

I know the reason for it, know why experimentation has to be so methodical, why results have to be repeatable under the exact same conditions. I know all that, can appreciate the logic behind it, and the fact that emotions don't enter the equation at all.

But that doesn't mean I like doing the same damn thing day in and day out. Even it is for the greater good. For *our* greater good.

Even Addison, one of the most dedicated people I know, looks like she's ready to move past the meteor glass and back onto the writs. I can't blame her either. Deciphering that language we found in the City seems like a much more stimulating endeavor than continuing to stare at this glass.

Besides, why do we have to assume everything on Tajss has some hidden frequency that the Zmaj can harness as a resource? Once they figured out the regular meteor glass can be used to power the old technology, it's like we've decided that the sky will continue to rain miracles down on a regular basis!

It doesn't make a whole lot of sense, but we all seem to go along with it. Including me, I guess.

"What brings you to the city?" I ask Sarah, pulling my thoughts out of the downward spiral.

The weight lifts from my shoulders the moment we step out of the lab doors.

"I was checking in with Rosalind on my way back from the mining settlement," she explains. "I'll head back to the caves right after this. Drosdan is waiting for me so we can head out."

I'm sure he is. If there's one thing I've noticed with all the Zmaj-human matings, it's that the Zmaj are both protective and possessive of their mates. They don't like to spend time away from them, which none of the women seem to mind. In fact, they seem to have a glow to them, which is nice to see.

"How's the mining settlement?" I ask.

She frowns, shaking her head.

"Same," she says, resignation in her voice.

That settlement happened before my time here in the City. Apparently there was some douchebag named Gershom who led a Zmaj hate campaign that a lot of the humans fell in with. No one talks about it much, at least in the City, but what I gather is he was a grade-A tool. Dead now, but the remnants of his followers live in a settlement southeast of the City.

"They still hating on the Zmaj?" I ask.

"Not so much hating. They're scared," she sighs, motioning futilely with her hands. "I don't know what it will take to get them over it."

"Fear is a powerful emotion," I agree.

"Yeah, no matter how many times the Zmaj have saved them, brought them supplies, everything really, they're still frightened. They don't show it, not as much as they did, but it's there."

"Maybe in time they'll get over it," I force a smile.

Sarah nods. The corners of her lips strain up but her eyes

narrow and twitch and a vein on her forehead throbs, giving away the lie. What else can we do? Some people need to accept reality. We're on Tajss, our home. The generation ship we were all supposed to live and die on crashed. It's over, face reality, kids. This is it. Kind of like my having to go to work every day in a lab. It's not the life I dreamed of, ever.

"City is looking better," she says, clearly changing the subject.

"Yeah, Rosalind has several crews doing nothing but cleanup," I say.

"That's been going on for a while. Lot of work," she says.

"Probably more than we'll ever see done," I say. A bit morbid but it's true.

"Unfortunately," Sarah says. "These Invaders aren't helping anything either."

"Yeah," I agree. "It's not as if Tajss was bad enough without the extra threats… oh wait, it was."

She chuckles at my dark joke.

"Desert planet, check. Blasted wasteland, check. Some of the deadliest flora anyone could ever dream up, check," she smiles, ticking off items on her fingers.

"Don't forget the shipwreck that stranded us here in the first place," I grin, holding up a finger.

"I guess it's just like Dr. Malcolm says in *Jurassic Park*. Life does find a way," she says.

"I've never seen that one," I say.

"Really? I loved those vids," she says.

"Nah, wasn't my thing. *Firefly*, now there's a show I could get into," I say. "That second season…"

"So many people talk about it, but I never did see it," she sighs. "Apparently I really missed out."

"Oh God you have!" I exclaim, blood rushing in my ears.

Sarah and I chat a little more, but part ways when we reach the building Rosalind's office is located in. A massive fountain dominates the center of the square, in the middle of which sits a huge stone statue of a Zmaj. The basin has water in it now and is the central place everyone comes to get their supply of that precious resource.

The fountain is one of a handful of very rare remnants of art that survived the "Devastation" as the Zmaj call it. It's evidence of a past that is mostly lost. The Zmaj who survived it have spotty memories at best.

The epis plant that all of us humans also take now helps us adapt to the harsh climate here, but it also lengthens lifespans. The Zmaj we've encountered have lived a long, long time. None of them seem to know how long it's been. Their answers are vague at best. The trauma of everything that happened left them with large chunks of missing memory.

"I've got to go," Sarah says. "Rosalind is in her office and Drosdan is waiting for me."

"Thanks for the company," I say.

"No probs!" She waves, then turns and walks off toward the edge of the city.

The protective dome that covers the City sparkles in the distance. The dome not only keeps out the innumerable predators that roam Tajss looking for something to eat, but it also filters out some of the double red suns' rays. Which means it's only steaming hot underneath it, not boiling.

Taking a deep breath, I hold it for a second, then exhale slowly. As I reach for the door my hand trembles. Nerves? Seriously? I know Rosalind. It's not like she's *that* intimidating.

Okay, well, she is, sure. It's not that, though. I want this. I don't know what *this* is but I want it. Change, any change, to the boring monotony that my life has become. Rosalind is the center of the budding political scene here on Tajss. That would be an interesting area to be in! Sarah is off with

Drosdan now, so maybe Rosalind is looking for a new "right hand." Oh yes, please, dear god let it be that!

Okay, the Lady General has a lot on her plate. No point in keeping her waiting. Stepping through the door to the City's central command post I'm more than familiar with how to get to her office now. Here perhaps more than anywhere the work done on the City shows. Rosalind's office is several floors up and of course there are no elevators or lift tubes.

The stairs are almost all repaired. It's apparent where the construction teams have put in new material to replace what was missing. Glowing pieces of meteorite glass light up what otherwise would have been a nightmare to navigate. I can't imagine having done this before the glass and repairs.

Reaching her floor, the door is open when I get there, so I rap on it briefly before walking in. Two steps in and I stop, surprised to find Visidion sitting next to Rosalind.

His deep emerald eyes lock on me, and they seem to look right through me, straight to my soul. At first I thought the feeling was something that would go away with more exposure to the intimidating Zmaj, but it hasn't happened yet.

The Zmaj Tribe Commander has just as much presence as his beautiful mate, her queenly aura matching his intensity. They really are a good match. I can't imagine anyone besides him that could go toe to toe with Rosalind. She's demanding, imperial, and at times cold. She's a leader, through and through, but Visidion matches her while not being challenging. They're equals, in every sense of the word.

Hesitating, I look between the two of them. If they're both here, this must be an important meeting. The dim flicker of hope blooming in my stomach brightens. This has to be something big. It has to be! Biting my tongue hard enough to hurt, I keep an inappropriate grin from spreading across my face.

"Thanks for coming, Ashlee," Rosalinda murmurs,

gesturing for me to take a seat. "Please, sit down."

"Of course," I say taking the offered seat in front of them.

"How do you feel about putting your people skills to good use?" Visidion asks.

Don't smile, don't smile, don't smile.

The question is straight to the point while not explaining anything really.

"My people skills?" I ask, thoughts racing.

"Yes," Rosalind says, leaning forward. Her face is sincere and focused. "Would you be open to accompanying Nora and Archion to this group that he says he's from? The Order?"

My heart pounds and I'm lightheaded. It's hard to breathe. This! Accompany Nora and Archion back to the Order. I've heard rumors—everyone has—but to be asked to go?

A Zmaj showing up that isn't a part of the Tribe or living here in the City with us doesn't happen. Only a handful survived the Devastation, and those that did had become so primal that they couldn't stand to be around each other. Well, that was the common belief. The Tribe proved that wrong though.

Archion himself is an enigma. Gossip travels fast in our close-knit circles. I've heard how many times Archion has been a clinch player when he came across a group from the Tribe. Heck, he even helped us the last time we had Invaders sniffing around the perimeter of the city. He's one hell of a fighter with skills even the other Zmaj have commented on.

He's been nothing but helpful and he certainly doesn't have to be, especially after the Tribe Elders have been so suspicious of him.

I don't know that his intentions are completely pure either, but that doesn't mean that I don't hope they are really above reproach. That he's a good person, a hero who simply wanted to help. Maybe I'll be able to find that out and more.

It's obvious that he's a highly trained warrior. All the people who've seen him in action have commented on it. That combined with his references to this "Order" begs the question: what kind of training did he receive? Was it from this mysterious Order? Are they all as good as he is? And why are they so focused on fighting if they are? What objective do they have?

If only thinking of survival, I honestly don't think people would be spending so much time learning how to engage in battle. Case in point, the Zmaj who have joined us so far. Not that they aren't excellent warriors, but everything points to Archion being a cut above.

All of these thoughts run through my head quickly, a rapid-fire process that has me sitting up straighter. Man, this is so much better than I could have expected!

If I were alone, I'd likely be squeaking with delight, maybe dancing around my quarters, trying to expend this unexpected surge of energy. I might be out of that lab for a good period of time. That thought has me wanting to stand up and fist-punch the air, but I contain myself.

This is a kind of political advancement, and jumping up and down with joy won't exactly give Rosalind and Visidion confidence in my diplomatic abilities. This calls for a certain sense of gravitas and decorum. I don't want to lose the position before I get it.

Taking a deep, deliberate breath, I let it out slowly in an effort to calm myself. It's difficult, but I manage to hold in my exuberant reaction. Careful. They may be offering me the job, but I have to treat this like an interview.

"Yes, I would," I say. proud of how calm my voice sounds, forcing myself to accept their offer with just the right amount of ease.

I know people. If I act too eager, they may second-guess themselves. I need to be confident, contained. Not impressed at the opportunity. Inside though, it's a completely different story.

I'm going to be out of the lab! Wheeee!

"Wonderful," Rosalind says in that commanding voice that can hold a large crowd's attention. I've always admired it. "Just so you're clear on what we want—you are to act as a detached observer. You need to be able to compartmentalize how you feel in order to pick up details and facts about your surroundings and the people you meet. Because Nora is romantically involved with Archion, her opinion cannot be trusted. Not because we think she would be dishonest, but because her viewpoint simply can't be objective. She's compromised on that front."

"As she should be," Visidion inserts, glancing at Rosalind.

The corners of her lips rise slightly as she meets his eyes. Something passes between them, something real and strong. It's a brief moment, but there all the same before they turn their attention back to me.

"I understand," I nod, emphasizing that I do.

I wouldn't expect Nora to have a completely objective view on the matter, either. We're human, not robots without feelings and emotions. Even Visidion and Rosalind seem to be aware of that aspect of themselves.

"Good. We want you to gather data from the Order. No detail is too small. Also, to be clear, no one is to make any firm commitments. We're open to dealing with these new Zmaj, but we need to know more before we decide on anything permanent," Visidion adds.

Nodding, I see he's right. It's better to be cautious and protect ourselves. If this Order has the numbers and if they're all as well trained as Archion...

Leading them to our strongholds and letting them pass through our defenses... We could be overrun, our autonomy taken from us. Well, that's a bleak outlook, but not acknowledging that possibility would be dumb. If there's one thing I'm certain of, Rosalind and Visidion aren't dumb.

No, I'm glad that we're moving forward with caution. I didn't expect this assignment, but I also know that I'm the best woman for this job. I know people. I know how to deal with them, how to manipulate things when needed. I'm happy they see I have that skill set.

Maybe this is the turning point in my life. I can almost feel the shift around me as new possibilities and opportunities open. And it's an honor to be called before them for something like this. I'm grateful they noticed I could do more than work in the lab. The mind-numbing monotony could be over forever if I play my cards correctly and do this right.

"If you have time, we can have a late dinner tonight to discuss the details," Rosalind offers, standing up.

"That would be great," I agree, rising and turning to the door.

Before I take one step toward the door Nora bursts in, breathless, as if she ran all the way up. My mouth drops open and my chest constricts seeing her. Were her ears burning from how many times her name had been said during the meeting? Not that any of us were unkind, but still...

Looking at her I realize something is wrong, though. Her normally pretty, fresh face looks tired and drawn.

"What is it?" Rosalind asks, her voice sharp.

Her harsh tone is simply because she wants to help, and quickly. It's Rosalind's way. On the ship she was Lady General, leader of the armed forces, and she's used to people jumping at her commands. I've also seen her use it before to snap people out of a panic so that they can convey the issue efficiently.

"Something's wrong with Malcolm," Nora huffs. "They sent me to get you. Can you come with me?"

2

ASHLEE

*M*y blood runs cold and it's an effort of will to suppress a shiver. Malcolm? What could be wrong with Amara and Shidan's child?

"Yes," Rosalind agrees without hesitation, coming out from behind the desk. "Lead the way."

My stomach churns, bile rising in my throat. Uninvited, I follow Rosalind and Nora, breaking into a jog to keep up.

"Addison asked me to come to the city because Malcolm is having a continual stream of fevered nightmares with recurring imagery," Nora explains as we race down the stairs toward the nursery.

"Nightmares?" Rosalind asks.

"Yeah, maybe. It's gotten bad. Something needs to be done." She shakes her head grimly. "He's barely sleeping and it's taking a toll on him physically. He's only a child. He shouldn't have to be going through something this traumatic."

Nora is great with kids, which is why Addison would ask her to come. She's a regular Mary Poppins with a magical touch when it comes to the little ones. It's an impressive skill that goes beyond anything I've ever seen. I only hope that I will be half as good as her if I ever have a child.

I can't imagine what Amara and Shidan must be going through. The frustration of not being able to do anything while your baby suffers. If it's as bad as it seems, they must feel powerless. Sleep is supposed to be rejuvenating, a reprieve from everyday life to heal, not something to dread.

We race out of the main building and across the public square. Nora leads while Rosalind and I are right on her heels. The oppressive heat of the air outside presses down on us with a weight of its own. The nursery is inside a building only a block away from Rosalind's office. The moment we enter the building I hear the poor kid crying softly. When we enter, it breaks my heart to see him shivering in Amara's arms.

Addison is standing to next to Amara. She's pale and her face is drawn. It's obvious she's at her wits' end. There's a hint of relief when she sees us.

"You need to help my son right now!" Amara's shrill voice orders as soon as she sees us, her eyes red and hollow, the bags under them pronounced. White lines bracket her mouth, stress and worry clearly wearing on her.

Amara isn't known for being the most pleasant in the best of times, but in this situation I can't blame her for being bitchy. I'm sure I'd be an ass to everyone around if it were me. All things considered, she gets a pass.

Malcolm's weak crying is heartbreaking. It's like he doesn't have the energy left to be upset. He's quietly sobbing and crying, clinging to his mother.

Something shifts in the corner of my vision, startling me. Goosepimples race over my arms and I look for the threat with the hair on my arms standing on end. Hovering in the shadows of the corner is Archion, his sharp eyes watching everything. I've noticed that he doesn't miss much.

Rosalind speaks to Amara in a low, calm voice. It's obvious she's trying to keep the worried mother calm. I don't know if a calm voice will help with something like this, but I figure it can't hurt.

Poor Malcolm.

Normally he's full of life, but the robust child looks weak and his hair is stuck to his round face with sweat. The edges of his scales have a dull-gray tinge to them that doesn't look healthy at all. His eyes dart all around and he clings to Amara with a death grip.

What could he have seen? What is it that has him looking so... disturbed?

Whatever it is, he's too young to bear it well. Clenching my jaw, thoughts racing, I rub the back of my neck, desperate for some way I can help. About then Bashir walks into the room.

The big Zmaj—like they're all not huge comparative to any human—has an air about him. It's an air that's hard to explain, a presence he carries with him that makes me feel something I can only describe as reverence. He's serene, at peace with... well, everything. It's weird but nice to be around.

Bashir is also the resident voodoo doctor/mystic/high priest of Tajss. Or something like that. He's definitely the strangest of this strange world in which I live now. They've run tests on him, but the science only goes so far and doesn't explain him. He has premonitions and visions that are right way more than they're wrong, which is cool and creepy at the same time.

Is it telling that I'm relieved he's here?

It's an odd world where I can go from the monotony of the scientific method to looking to a witch doctor for help. At least he isn't wearing the skulls of his enemies around his neck or a headdress made of odd animal parts. Though that would be quite a look.

His leathery wing brushes my arm as he moves past and crouches next to Malcolm. The child looks even smaller with the seven-foot-tall alien next to him. Small and vulnerable.

"I hear you had some bad dreams," Bashir says in a low, gentle voice.

Malcolm nods, his eyes locking on Bashir's, focusing here and now for the first time since we arrived. He's reaching him.

"Yes," Malcolm replies, his voice so soft that it breaks my heart.

"What exactly did you see? Can you describe it?"

Malcolm is talking but his voice is so quiet I can't make out the words. I don't want to interrupt the one thing that seems to be helping, so I let my gaze wander around the room. Rosalind, Amara, and Shidan are all focused on Bashir and Malcolm, leaving nothing of interest in the room but Archion. The foreign Zmaj is frowning, his head tilted to one side, completely focused on Malcolm and Bashir. Suddenly his eyes widen and his mouth opens partway. He leaves the room without a word to anyone, pushing past me like I'm not there at all. Something in Malcolm's words triggered him, I'm sure, but what?

Part of me wants to run after him and question why he left. That's the less rational part though. My rational thoughts instantly realize how foolish that would be. Confronting a seven-foot-plus Zmaj who's a walking wall of muscle? Me? Alone? Yeah, not a bright idea. No, I'll file this away for future reference. If there's anything I've learned, it's that you can never have too much information about people.

I tune back into Malcolm's quiet voice, even more interested now to see what he has to say. If it affected Archion so strongly, I need to know. It might be relevant to this trip we're about to take. Still unable to hear him clearly, I move over to the position Archion left open.

"...and there were buildings that looked kind of sandy. And these things that have claws and tusks." He stops, frowning. "There's fighting, but I don't know why..."

I listen intently, though none of it makes much sense to me. The images are clearly disjointed, without a clear story or through-line. Not unexpected. He is speaking about a dream, or a series of dreams. They're never clear and straightforward, at least in my experience. I linger for a while anyway, curious and interested.

Rosalind touches my arm, surprising me by her sudden presence next to me.

"We should leave," she murmurs in a low voice.

It isn't an order, but I'm not going to ignore a suggestion from her either, so I nod. I glance back over my shoulder as we walk out, noting that Malcolm is much calmer now. He's sitting up in his mother's arms, his eyes are clearer, his voice stronger and steadier as Bashir questions him expertly. Even his scales are returning to their normally vibrant colors. Maybe he just needed to get all of it out to someone who might understand. I hope it helps long-term. Or at least that Bashir can keep helping him through it if he keeps being inundated by those dreams.

"I'll see you at dinner," Rosalind reminds me once we're outside.

"See you then," I agree.

My head aches as pressure builds, making it throb. Going from the high of the new position to seeing Malcolm so affected has me...out of sorts. My throat feels thick. Bouncing from the high of a new, much-wanted posting to Malcolm is hard. Mostly I feel bad for being so happy at a time like this.

I return to my quarters, trying to get back to my own center. I'm not all that successful. Closing the door behind me I lean against it and exhale, pinching the bridge of my nose to try and ease the pressure behind my eyes.

Right. It's not helping at all. Maybe being productive in a different way will help. I'm leaving to go on a trip of indeterminate length, so I need to clean this place. I get busy giving my space a deep cleaning to pass the time before I have to get ready for dinner. Rolling my sleeves up, I pick up the clothes I've left on the floor, change my sheets, and gather the trash to take out. By the time I'm done, I'm definitely in a better head space. And it's nice to see the place clean.

"Good job, girl," I mutter to myself, nodding in satisfaction.

It's almost time to leave, so I change into a nicer set of clothes, brush my hair the best I can with my makeshift brush that someone shaped out of animal bones, and head out.

On the ship, I used to take more time to get ready for things, applying makeup, wearing heels. In my experience, how you present yourself physically affects how people treat you. We don't have makeup or heels here and I wouldn't wear either even if we did. I'd sweat the makeup off in this heat and the idea of wearing heels when we could be attacked at any moment or when we have to walk so much...

Yeah, no thanks.

I guess there's a couple of things I don't miss from ship life. As I walk, my thoughts turns back to the interaction in the nursery. It plays through my mind like a scene from a vid-stick. I recall every detail as best I can in an effort to better reference it later. People tell you things—a lot of things—without realizing they're doing so. You have to be on your toes, ready to connect the dots when needed. And I have extra incentive to be vigilant now.

I want to show that I'm competent in this role, that Rosalind and Visidion can trust me. They'll be watching and assessing. I don't want to blow what might be my one chance to do something I really love.

By the time I make it to the intimate dining room, I have my game face on, my mind calm and focused. Dinner is already on the table, the scent of the food reminding me that I haven't eaten in quite a while. It's a modest affair with just a few offerings. Wine, smoked meat, and the famed sauce Delilah sends over from the Tribe from time to time that makes almost anything taste great. There's also some fresh-picked fruit that looks really good. Everything smells and looks delicious.

An image of when we first crash-landed on Tajss flashes through my thoughts. Hurt, starving, dying of thirst, literally. I didn't think then that we had a chance of surviving. We've come a long way.

I try hard to never forget that, to never stop appreciating what we've managed to carve out here on this alien planet, to never forget it could be worse.

"Welcome," Rosalind says, extending her hand.

"Thanks," I say, looking around.

It's a small affair with only a handful of people attending. Rosalind and Visidion are here of course, and so is Archion and Nora. The surprise guest is Ladon. I'm not sure why I'm surprised he's here—he's the "OG" of the Zmaj, sort of. He's not the oldest but the City was his territory before our ship crashed and got the Zmaj to get over their territorial ways.

Mostly. They still get tense with each other sometimes, something primal that they call the bijass. I can't even pretend to understand what it is, but I've seen it affect them and it's not pretty. It's actually scarier to see one of them in the grips of it is than most of the things on the planet that are trying to kill you. Yeah, I'd rather face a zemlja, one of the giant sand worms that burrow their way around the planet than a Zmaj in the grip of the bijass.

It's a small, obviously calculated group so that we can all talk to each other rather than naturally breaking off. I'm sure it's intended to help Nora, Archion, and me to build a rapport. Definitely has Rosalind's touch all over it.

We sit down to the dinner and the conversation starting smoothly enough. The topics are deliberately light, but it soon turns to the task at hand, the reason why we're here.

"Archion, how long will it take to reach the Order's territory?" Rosalind inserts neatly during a lull.

The fork in his hand stops midway to his mouth and his shoulders tense. He doesn't say anything for a second, but it's a long telling second. Yeah, there's a lot going on in there.

"Two to five days," Archion responds, deliberately vague. "It depends on how quickly we travel."

"And they won't attack if you bring strangers with you?" Visidion presses.

That would be...really unfortunate. No way the three of us could fight against even two Zmaj, even if they're not as trained as Archion. There's another long pause as he swallows, frowning. That's not reassuring, and when he speaks, it's not better.

"We will not pass across the boundaries without permission," he responds carefully.

Clearly choosing his words. There's no doubt we all notice it, but Rosalind and Visidion only nod.

"I see," Visidion says, nodding.

"So this mission may not take place at all?" Rosalind asks, her sharp eyes taking in everything.

"It will be what it will be," Archion says, setting his fork down on his plate.

Forks are something we humans introduced to the Zmaj. Random, I know, but watching him picking his words carefully, studying his body language, it stands out to me for some reason. They used to use a wood thing to eat with that was almost a cross between a knife and a spoon. It was weird and hard to use without cutting your mouth if you didn't have scales to protect it from the sharp edges.

"So, you have no way of getting an okay before you go?" Rosalind asks.

Oh, that's clever.

Archion's eyes lock onto her, his frown deepening as he sees through her question. The air is heavy as tension builds like a storm is about to let loose.

"It will be what it will be," he repeats, each word dropping like a stone into still water.

"I'm sure it will all be fine," Nora says, placing a hand on his arm.

He doesn't take his eyes away from Rosalind, but something about him softens at her touch. It isn't something I can pinpoint to a specific change or difference. It's good to know she has that effect on him. It means he's still—under all his secrecy and training—a Zmaj like the rest of them. If there's one thing I know about the Zmaj, their "treasures" take precedence over all.

"I'd like more than airy assurances," Rosalind says. Her voice has a dangerous edge, but this time Visidion touches her arm and I watch the same interplay in reverse.

"Archion," Visidion says. "Will you guarantee the safety of those we send with you?"

Archion shifts his attention slowly off of Rosalind to Visidion. He's glaring, but Visidion meets his glare with an open frankness that cuts through it. The glare fades as the corners of Archion's mouth soften.

"I do," he says.

"That is all we can ask," Visidion nods.

Rosalind fairly thrums with anger but doesn't say a word. She nods, her frown deep, and I notice a vein pulsing next to her left eye.

I don't know if Nora and Archion have worked out a signal for when he wants to leave or if she can sense things might take a turn into truly uncomfortable territory, but she times her exit perfectly.

"I'm sorry—I'm beyond exhausted from today. And we need our sleep for our journey tomorrow."

"Yes, Nora is correct," Archion agrees on the heels of her polite excuse. He stands with her, nodding at the table. "Dinner was lovely. My thanks."

"Of course," Rosalind murmurs, her eyes watchful.

They track the couple as they leave together, her expression unreadable. Hmmm. I get the distinct feeling Archion is trying to force himself past some point of hesitation, some hang up he can't push through. Maybe it's something as simple as doubt that his brothers will agree to a trade or ally deal with us. That would make sense, but it seems there could be more behind it. I guess only time will tell.

He's telegraphing some kind of a lack of confidence in this endeavor. It doesn't bode well for the trip, though we're going one way or another. After they leave, we finish the meal in a heavy silence.

I don't know about everyone else, but my mind is firmly on tomorrow. Will we be successful? How dangerous is this mission? Of course, it's dangerous, we're on Tajss, but I can't help feeling that the real trouble I'll be facing isn't going to be from the normal run-of-the-mill beast or plant trying to eat me.

"Thank you for the meal," Ladon says, having finished his plate. "It was a most... enlightening evening. Ashlee, I wish you the best on your journey. I'm sure it will prove fruitful."

"Thank you," I say, cheeks warming.

"Of course," he says, then he walks to the door.

"I should be going too," I say, rising from the table.

"Ashlee," Rosalind says. "A moment, if you don't mind."

She's watching Ladon leaving, not me. When the door closes, she puts her full attention on me. Rosalind has this look that makes you feel like you're under a microscope. There's nothing she misses, and you know it. It's powerful, and I fully admit I'm jealous.

"What are your general thoughts on Archion?" Rosalind asks, propping her chin up on her fist.

"Yes, we are interested in knowing what you think of him," Visidion adds, his eyes focused in that laser-sharp way he has.

I think carefully before I respond, despite the pressure to simply blurt something out under their expectant looks. I don't want to get anyone in trouble or say things out of turn without enough information. It's too dangerous, so I keep my answer diplomatic.

"He seems sincere, if...not at liberty to divulge too much."

Rosalind nods, silently waiting. I know the technique, but damn it if it's not effective. The urge to squirm in my seat, to blurt out all my thoughts, is almost overwhelming. Almost, but this is my arena too, so I hold myself still, meeting her gaze.

Finally she breaks her gaze with me and looks at Visidion. A silent exchange passes between them and it ends with him giving the slightest of nods.

"We agree," Rosalind says, speaking softly, almost as if she's not talking to me anymore. "Be careful when you're with him. There's more to this than we know."

"I will," I say, taking a deep breath and letting the pressure of their scrutiny flush away with it.

Time will complete the story. Speculation can only nix a potentially powerful alliance before we even have the chance to build it. Keeping hope alive is the goal.

At least for now.

3

KHAL

*L*eaping up and spreading my wings, I use them to lighten my weight on the sand. Cresting another dune I scour the desert, looking for any sign of my brother's passage.

Nothing.

Only more sunbaked red sand. Clenching my jaw, I continue searching with a growing desperation that I struggle to rein in. Where is Archion? This is not at all like my brother and not at all like the responsible mentor and leader he is.

Rubbing my face I try to ignore the burning in my chest as both my hearts seem to be consumed in acid. It takes all my will not to let my dark thoughts come to the front. What if he's...

No. I will not let the negative thoughts take hold. It is not possible that my brother could have met a terrible fate. It simply is not.

Archion has been at the very top of the warrior line for decades on this side of Tajss. An inarguable, objective fact. He has a risen so high among the ranks that he reports directly to the Council and only to the Council. Nobody else.

That Tashak has sent me to look for him is...troublesome, but the Seers aren't known for their patience and Archion is already unforgivably late. If he returns without a limb or maimed in some other horrifying way, he might be forgiven, but it will be a long time before he is seen in the revered fashion he has enjoyed for so long.

Harsh, yes, but it is a fact. That would be a bad enough end, but if he has...

Shaking my head I continue my forward momentum, scanning the area around me constantly while I think. There is no scenario where he would betray the Order. After a lifetime spent protecting and upholding our values and objectives, it's not possible.

Archion is above reproach. I refuse to even entertain the notion. Clenching my jaw, I ruthlessly cut off my thoughts. It's not a productive line of reasoning. Focus on the search, no matter how mind-numbing it is to see the same, barren desert giving me no signs, no reason to hope. This is why we train. Keeping attention focused, missing nothing, seeing all is the heart of being a warrior.

The suns reach their zeniths, beating down and raising the temperature. I cover the sand as quickly as possible, the scorching light a familiar burn against my scales left exposed by my robes. I follow the search grid I planned and memorized before I left. The painstaking method was chosen so I do not miss anything by accident.

Yes, it takes more time, but it is better to be thorough the first time rather than having to retrace my footsteps. Not that it has mattered much thus far. As carefully as I look, I do not see tracks or any sign that the Order-marked rifts have been used.

No sign that anything larger than a small animal has been

anywhere near here. The longer this takes the more the emptiness in my stomach grows, threating to consume everything. Growing larger and heavier, but I will not give in to that black pit of despair.

Archion is still here. My brother will return. There is no other option.

Suddenly there's an odd sensation in my midsection as I mentally proclaim this. It's like a tugging in my gut. An answer?

Turning, the gentle but insistent pull grows stronger. When I move in that direction the feeling becomes so distinct, I know I'm on the correct course.

"He is alive." I whisper the words out loud, willing them to be so.

No, more than that, needing them to be so. I follow the feeling, holding onto it as tightly as I can. It is the only hope that I have had for days upon days. I need it, need the fuel it provides.

A renewed sense of purpose combines with a surge of energy, the two aiding me in traveling fast while keeping my eyes sharp. The suns drop to the horizon while I search, clinging to my renewed hope, but it does not matter. I don't find anything, no signs of his passage. No signs of struggle, nothing that says anyone has been this way for a long, long time.

The shadows grow longer, the suns dipping below the horizon. My stomach sinks as I have to admit that it is too late to stay out much longer. Without the bright suns out during the day to guide me, I could miss tracks or other signs even if I come upon them. That would not only set me back in my search but could lead me astray.

Struggling with my desire to find my brother, I finally force myself to turn back. I want to keep searching, keep looking until my body gives way, but I can't make decisions based on emotions. That would be rash and stupid and it will not serve any purpose, and most especially I won't find Archion doing it.

Turning away from the empty sands I race the setting suns back. The Order's home is well hidden. If I didn't know what I was looking for, I'd never find the entrance. It's covered over with sand and a small stone marker.

Lowering the trap door over my head, I walk along the hand-hewn tunnel and bring the raging storm of my thoughts under control. Simple breathing exercises calm the storm, so simple it's one of the earliest things I recall learning when I was but a child.

The Order has been my home since my earliest memories. Archion and I grew up under its careful tutelage. Memories are dim, foggy recollections because the past doesn't matter. Right now is all that one should have their attention on.

By the time I reach the end of the tunnel and emerge into the empty room at its end, my emotions are under control, carefully hidden underneath a lifetime of training. The door slams closed over the tunnel entrance as the door to the room opens and the two guards with lochabers at the ready look in, silently challenging.

I signal with my hand that all is well and I'm alone. They nod, stoic as befits their post. Pushing past them I make my way to Tashak, ready to report my failure. The Council Seer is walking down the hall leaving the meeting rooms when I run into him.

"Khal," he says, greeting me warmly.

I stop, press my fist into my open hand and give him a half-bow, showing my respect to an Elder of the Council. He nods his acceptance brusquely.

"What did you find?" he asks.

"Nothing," I say, focusing on the ground between us.

Surprisingly he places a consoling hand on my shoulder. It startles me into looking up and meeting his eyes. His jewel-toned robes rustle with the movement, his staff still held firmly in his other hand. Glancing at that strong hand, I breathe in deeply and swallow the lump in my throat, refusing to entertain the thought that I am certain the Seer is building up toward.

"I know he is still alive," I say, preempting him. I cannot allow him to say the words. I place my hand over my midsection. "I feel it here."

I try to convey the feeling, the surety, in an effort to convince him. If he says what I fear, I won't be allowed to continue my search. When the Seer nods, I can see that he may be humoring me.

"Only time will tell us what has happened to Archion," he replies after a brief pause. "We will wait and see."

The words are neutral, but the tone is not. He frowns, the slightest hint of danger or perhaps trepidation lacing the statement and his expression. It is clear that he would rather the former be true than the latter, but the latter is not possible. My brother is alive.

I feel it inside, a knowing that will not be denied. And I refuse to believe otherwise. No matter what any Seer tells me.

4

ASHLEE

"Almost ready. Just need to give it one final go over," Addison says.

"Got it," I say.

I step back from the rover and take a moment to truly appreciate the vehicle. It beats trudging through the sand in the desert, feet sinking in with every step. Even though the Zmaj are larger and weigh much more than us, they have a way easier time traveling out there, their wings giving them enough lift to skim over the sand rather than sink into it.

It's pretty amazing to watch. I've been green with jealousy more than a few times watching them glide over a stretch I know I'm going to be gasping for breath after, but it is what it is. At least they introduced us to epis. Yeah, it's addictive—fatally so if you don't get your dose—but I don't think we would survive in these harsh conditions without it. I still remember the cool burst of relief after first taking it. And how much healthier I felt instantly.

It does weird me out to think that it's literally changing us on a cellular level, so I try not to dwell on it too much. The addiction part is a downside, but even if we were to find a way off this planet, where would we go?

Our original destination, the planet we were supposed to colonize after generations spent on the ship, is still way too far to reach within our lifespan. I suppose we could just stick to the original plan if we were able to build a ship, but it doesn't seem smart to risk something with a high chance of failure when we can build a life here. *Have* built a life here.

And I don't want the children to have to go from playing outside to being trapped in a ship like we were.

"Hey Nora, I want to check in on Malcolm before we head out," I say. "I'll be right back."

"Sure," Nora says, pausing in helping Addison and Archion in loading the vehicle.

"I'll tag along," Maeve offers.

"Great!" I agree.

I've been thinking about the boy since I first saw his strained little face. I hope he's doing better now.

"Have you heard anything?" I ask Maeve as we walk.

She shakes her head.

"Maybe that's a good thing," she points out. "It isn't like his mother is one to keep any problems to herself. If Malcolm was doing badly, we likely would have heard about it."

"That's for sure," I snort. "Amara being quiet would be a huge indicator."

I'm a little guilty over agreeing with the assessment about the overwhelmed mother, but it's really been true of her since I've known her. When we turn into the hall leading to the nursery, my steps falter for a moment. Maeve and I exchange a hopeful glance at the happy giggle that travels down toward us. Hurrying the rest of the way, we duck into the room to find a completely different child inside.

Laughing and playing with his toys while still in bed

recovering, Malcolm is almost back to his normal, happy self. My chest expands as joy blooms in my heart at the sight of him. No child should look as traumatized as he looked when we last saw him. Now he's obviously been recently scrubbed clean, dressed in new pajama bottoms, his eyes bright and cheeks a healthy pinkish-tan.

His tiny wings flutter when he looks up as we enter. He grins and waves, his bright smile infectious.

"Hi Ashlee! Hi Maeve!"

"Hi Malcolm," I grin as I cross over to him and ruffle his soft hair between his budding horns. "Glad to see you doing better."

The rush of relief that I feel could only be a fraction of what Amara must be feeling. Amara is sitting to the side, still watching with a hawk eye, but the lines of worry on her face have relaxed. Good.

Addison walks over, already there to check on Malcolm as well.

"He's doing so much better," I observe.

"One more thing to thank the hidden gods of Tajss for," Addison returns with a smile, a twinkle glimmering in her eye.

Maeve and I both chuckle at the joke. Though I guess it isn't really fully a joke. Too many things have happened that point toward something more than we can explain.

Meteor showers that strike exactly at the right time to stop Invader attacks; the resulting glass from their showers when we needed to figure out a way to power the old technology on Tajss; the prophetic dreams and visions that have affected more than just Malcolm.

It's a lot to try to ignore wholesale, for me anyway. Doesn't mean that I buy into everything, just that...I'm keeping my mind open in the face of evidence.

"The divinity of Tajss is nothing to joke about." Bashir's serious, deep voice comes as a surprise to all three of us.

Sharing an "oops" glance, I turn to him.

Almost as one we incline our heads quietly, mockingly obedient to his serious words. I like and respect Bashir, but he needs to loosen up, at least sometimes. If we were all serious about everything all the time, we'd go crazy. Levity in the face of looming danger, of unexplained events that don't quite fit in the neat box we've lived our lives in so far, is a natural release mechanism.

Bashir doesn't get irritated but sighs in response to our teasing, turning his attention firmly to Malcolm. I sober as he walks over to the bed and leans down next to the little boy. I'm again struck by the massive size difference between the two, but that isn't what keeps my attention. The strangest thing happens as all of us watch.

The small boy and Bashir lock eyes, watching each other intently from only a couple of feet away. The small hairs on my arms stand up as I watch, an odd current in the air around them. I'm certain I'm not the only one feeling it. Everyone else's eyes are riveted on the scene too.

Nothing big happens. Nothing that I could point at later with definitive proof of anything. Bashir's face stays mostly neutral while everything in him focuses on Malcolm, but the child doesn't have the same discipline as the older Zmaj. Various expressions flicker across his soft face as Malcolm stares, like he's listening to something only he hears.

A cold shiver taps up my spine, a chill of reaction. Malcolm nods slowly, frowning, at something only he can hear.

He shakes his head. Watching, I distinctly feel left out of whatever interaction they're having. I can't deny something is passing between the mismatched pair. It almost looks like they're...having a conversation, one without any words. Well, without any spoken words. A telepathic conversation?

It sounds crazy, but... here we are, aren't we?

On this crazy planet where it seems like so much more is possible than there ever was on the ship only a few short years ago. Neither Bashir nor Malcolm say anything to indicate that they're talking to each other, but watching the interaction from the sidelines...

I don't know how else to explain it.

Even if Bashir was just pretending, Malcolm is too young to simply play along without clear direction, and why would Bashir do something like that anyway?

I can't see it, not with a child who went through something very real to him. It's something to think about. Watching, I file away the experience with all the other information I've gathered in the mental cabinet labeled "shit I can't explain." It's getting kind of full in there.

I watch a little longer until it feels too much like I'm intruding on what should be a private moment. Looking at Maeve, I nod and she responds the same, deciding silently that it's our cue to leave. The rover should be ready to go soon anyway.

We leave the nursery as quietly as possible, though I honestly don't know if anything would break that locked-in stare between Bashir and Malcolm. We stroll back waiting for word that it's time to go.

"Have any idea what was going on back there between Malcolm and Bashir?" I ask.

I'd noticed an odd look on Maeve's face when she took in the interaction. Not that I blame her. It *was* odd. She sighs, looking around as if to make sure nobody else is within listening distance. Instinctively I look around too.

"Unless someone has bat hearing, I think we're good," I say softly, stepping closer.

She smiles briefly, but it fades as she leans down toward me, lowering her voice anyway. I lean in to make sure I catch every word of her quiet voice. Whatever she's going to say, it's clear she doesn't want anyone else to overhear it.

"I'm not sure exactly what was going on back there, but..." She stops, hesitating.

"But what?" I prompt. "I wouldn't have brought it up if I didn't think something was going on."

She nods, biting her lip.

"Yeah, you're right." She clears her throat, stepping even closer until she's almost whispering in my ear. "There...might be more going on than we can see." I follow her hand motion as she gestures down to her ribs. "Ever since that meteorite glass fused with my ribs...Padraig and I share dreams."

Tilting my head to one side, my pulse quickens.

"You share dreams?" I repeat, making sure I heard her correctly.

I wasn't expecting her to share such an intimate piece of information. She nods, a flush creeping across her checks, her chin dipping down, but she doesn't stop. She crosses her arms over her chest in an almost protective gesture, then plows on with what she has to say.

"I know it sounds crazy, but we do. And the dreams aren't the only change since then. We've also developed a telepathic...sense I guess you would call it. A... knowing. A feeling that sometimes blooms into visions that we can't quite understand. At least not yet." She shakes her head, her gaze turning distant. "I know how it sounds, but I'm at a point now that I just can't hide it." Her eyes focus on me again. "And I don't know if I should, not with everything else that's happening." She turns to look back toward the nursery, nodding in its direction. "Case in point."

Cupping my elbow with one hand I tap my lips, thinking hard on what she shared. I turn this new information over, examining it in the light of everything else I've heard and seen. It sounds crazy. If we were on the ship it would sound completely bonkers, but we're not on the ship anymore.

We're on Tajss. After everything I've seen here, it doesn't sound so impossible, not anymore. That's a good indication of exactly how far down the rabbit hole all of us already are.

"I believe you," I tell Maeve as we resume walking. I can't stop myself glancing around, but we still seem to be alone. Even if anyone is watching us, we look like we are chatting about something as inane as the weather. "We've all seen some crazy stuff."

She chuckles quietly, exhaling heavily. Her face relaxes as she shakes her head and drops her arms back to her sides.

"Isn't that the truth," she grimaces. "Sometimes I wonder if my past self would even recognize me."

"I hear you."

Fact is, experiences change people, and we've all been through some intense events at this point. No way could we all come out the same on the other end. I ponder that as we settle into a comfortable silence. But my thoughts switch over to the topic we just discussed.

I don't know if she's thinking about everything she just said, but I can't help but try to look at her experience in terms of the bigger picture and what I already know.

Whatever is happening with Padraig, Bashir, and the dragonlings is fascinating. New and uncharted, it's something beyond the purely scientific, beyond what we've been taught to expect from the world.

That doesn't mean it's any less valid though, only something we don't quite understand yet. Something that could turn everything we think we know on its head. I push that thought away to think over later. There are more finite, relevant particulars to focus on now.

Like Malcolm's dreams. I wonder how they tie in with

Archion? What in them caused him to react the way he did? There is no doubt in my mind his reaction was in response to what the little boy described in his dreams.

Unfortunately, I don't think asking Archion directly would get me anywhere. He holds everything close to the chest. And it might make him close up even more to ask something so pointed, to poke at something that's clearly a sensitive spot. That really wouldn't help right now, not when I'm going to be spending so much time around him on this trip.

More than that I'm going to have to rely on him both to get us to the Order safely, and maybe to protect both Nora and me while we're there. Once there, I have no idea what to expect.

I can't face the subject head-on, but I know there's something going on with those dreams that he's not being open about. I'm going to have to practice patience while working at this puzzle. Luckily, I know how to play my cards right when opportunities present themselves.

I'll take a cue from Archion and hold my thoughts close, for now. Shoving my hands into my pockets, a smile forms on my face as a lightness blooms in my chest. This trip is starting to look more and more interesting.

I can't wait.

5

KHAL

The younger Zmaj's cobalt-blue eyes widen with the realization he moved a fraction too slowly to avoid my blow.

Good. He's learning to gauge the ebb and flow of battle, but that doesn't mean that I hold back, however. His head snaps back from the force of my blow and he stumbles, then using his tail to buy himself room by swiping at me, rolls to his side and stops in a crouch.

He turns his head and spits blood onto the sand floor of the training space. I can't suppress a grin. There's fire in this one. Good. I wouldn't hold back anyway. The only way to improve is to be beaten by those better than you. The thousands of bruises I've had from Archion and my other brothers taught me that well. If I hold back it will only slow him, which will not help anyone.

Still, I let him rise to his feet. He watches me, cautiously wary, as he should be. He touches his jaw, rubbing where I hit him, then he nods. His hands tighten on his lochaber, wings flutter, and his weight shifts onto the balls of his feet.

It's too obvious. He must be better. I lower my lochaber,

opening myself, inviting him in with an apparent opening in my defenses. Foolishly, he takes the bait, but it's what I predicted. His speed is impressive. He races in, lochaber low, cutting up toward my jaw.

I see the certainty on his face. He believes he has found an advantage. His commitment to his action is impressive, if stupid. Sliding to one side I rap him hard on the wrist with the blunt end of my lochaber, sending his weapon flying away.

It lands in the sand with a muted thud, but I only peripherally hear it. I'm focused, more focused than I ever remember being in a battle. All my frustrations rise within me and I attack. Laser-point strikes, blow after blow landing exactly where they will do the most good.

He dodges but I hit two out of three times. There is a harried look in his eyes. He was not expecting such speed or such precision. In truth, I have never been more precise before. My mind and body are one, my arms and legs moving almost of their own accord, thoughts and actions melding seamlessly, tirelessly.

My muscles thrum with the thrill of it. I could fight forever. I could fight an entire army myself and emerge victorious. It's a foolish thought, I know, but I am drunk on this new state—the root of which I know. I refuse to think too deeply of what is fueling my power.

He ducks, slips, and rolls to the side, barely avoiding my downward swing. The blade of my lochaber cuts into the ground where he was a second prior. He scrambles backward, trying to get away. There's desperation on his face but more fear. The scent of it fills my nostrils. He stumbles across his dropped lochaber, grips it tight while leaping up and back, using his tail and wings to put some distance between us.

He lands lightly but he knows he's beat. Defeat screams

from his posture, the slump of his shoulders, the tremble of the lochaber in his hands. He's no longer fighting to win but for the dim hope of surviving my wrath.

Enough. It's time to finish this. It isn't right to take out my frustration on him. I feint a forward attack then shift to the left. I strike three times, once on the shoulder, another on his forearms, and one precise, hard blow to his thigh. He drops his lochaber and his leg buckles. As he falls his uninjured hand scrambles for his knife, only to find the sheath empty.

I flip his knife around in my free hand and lay its sharp edge against the skin of his throat. As his pulse beats hard against the unforgiving edge of his own blade, his eyes lock with mine. He swallows carefully, staring at me.

I do not move. Do not give an inch, waiting.

"I concede defeat," he says carefully, his voice low as he attempts not to press further into the knife. "I concede."

There. The end. I nod sharply, stepping back.

"Good fight," I say automatically, flipping the knife once again in my hand so the hilt is facing out.

I offer him his weapon back. His hand is shaking as he retrieves his knife, sliding it back into its sheath. I turn to leave him to his humiliation.

"I appreciate the sentiment, but it's clear I'm not skilled enough," he responds with calm humility.

Turning my head to look back at him I laugh, a barking, unexpected sound.

"True enough," I agree, turning back to him. "Yet."

I appreciate that he isn't allowing his resounding defeat to overwhelm him.

"Thank you for taking time to offer your instruction," he says, planting a fist into the open palm of his other hand and bowing so low he's almost doubled over.

He'll do well, in time. Before I can continue the conversation, a hush falls over the assembled crowd. Following the gazes of those in my line of sight, I turn toward one of the tunnels leading into the practice ground. The jewel-toned robes identifies the approaching figure as one of the Council.

As the figure emerges into the light I realize it's Tashak.

Why is he here? Why would one of the Council deign to appear at a routine practice?

I watch as he closes with the rest of the fighters. His appearance alone is enough to halt the sparring matches, rows of flowing robes coming to a standstill as the other Zmaj stop to watch in silence. Waiting to see what will happen. I'm not surprised. A high enough rank can stop any activity flat.

In moments it becomes clear he is making his way to me. I keep my face neutral, wondering what we could have to speak about so soon after our last conversation. Is there news of my brother? My hearts dance in their cage, my blood running hot.

As he comes up to me I place one fist in my palm and bow without taking my eyes off of his. Respectful but not overly. He nods his head in acknowledgment, his deep amethyst eyes calm and in control.

"What brings you to the training grounds, Councilor?" I ask politely when he does not immediately launch into his purpose.

My patience is thin and even with one so far above me, I have little to spare.

"I wish to discuss your impressive service, Khal," he replies.

He glances around at the large number of eyes trained upon him. It doesn't faze him to be the center of attention. It seems clear, to me at least, that he relishes in it. The color at the edges of his scales deepens and he pitches his voice to be heard by all of them.

I don't. A prickle runs along my scales, a slightly uncomfortable itch formed by so many eyes on me at once. I replay his words, thinking. Discuss my impressive service. I don't have to be particularly sensitive to understand it is a clear and deliberate insinuation. The Council is considering me for a promotion.

"I see," I reply on autopilot.

I do not know what else to say. My brain is almost at a complete standstill at the unexpected topic. My feelings are...mixed. I never thought my reaction to such a discussion would be so lackluster, but it's difficult to ignore the reason why this discussion is happening.

My brother was my hero. No, *is*. I've always regarded him with a heady mixture of awe, admiration, and love. He cannot have simply...disappeared. No, he is too skilled. Archion is a powerful force. Impossible to defeat—a truth I'm well acquainted with. The trainee I bested has no idea. Archion is twice the warrior.

"Your skills in combat are formidable," Tashak continues when I don't elaborate. "As is your strategic mind. We believe..."

I listen, attempting to fully absorb the words, though my attention is halfhearted. I've been eager to rise in the ranks for a long-time, frustrated at always being delegated to act as support rather than as a lead. It's been my singular goal, but not like this. I've never wanted to replace Archion but instead sought to fight at his side, to be his equal in the eyes of our brethren.

No, I don't like what this discussion signifies. The weight it carries, what caused it to occur at all. I know it's not because the Council suddenly noticed I have the ability. I'm not so egotistical that I can believe that. The timing is too telling.

It's Archion. Where is he? He's been gone too long. Saying

41

it or not, they're writing him off as lost. I can't do that, not yet. I want him back more than I want any kind of promotion or recognition from the Council.

I have dreamed of this moment for so long, year after year, but now that I am receiving it...

I'm hollow. Empty inside, my mouth dry as if I were the one taking in mouthfuls of sand and not my erstwhile opponent.

"... a promotion is long overdue. You will be promoted to full Scout, with all the requisite honors of this..."

He continues talking, but my thoughts wander and I'm only dimly aware of what he's saying. When he finishes he places a hand on my shoulder. Twice in as many days he's touched me in such a friendly manner. Meeting his eyes, I see the truth written there.

He hasn't announced it, but the Council has decided. They're not adding a Scout, they're replacing one.

"Congratulations," he says, smiling broadly.

His hand tightens on my shoulder and he exerts pressure, turning me to face the assembled warriors of the Order. They cheer and applaud, slamming their tails against the packed sound. It's deafeningly loud. I turn to Tashak and salute, then turn to the warriors and repeat the gesture. They applaud louder.

Tashak lets me go and walks away. The warriors come forward, slapping my back, shaking my hand, all of them happy and congratulatory. I play my part, accepting their well-wishes, but I'm distant from it. Disconnected, like it's happening to someone else. I'm a puppet going through the motions.

When the last of them have come and had their say, I slip out of the training grounds and climb the surrounding wall. Staring at my home across the roofs of our hidden dwellings.

It was a strategic decision to hollow out parts of this cliff for our outpost. The homes and communal buildings beyond the cliff itself are made out of sand and stone. From a distance, the village blends into its surroundings, hidden, camouflaged from danger.

Multiple staircases lead up to the various levels and rounded doorways, dome-shaped dwellings situated next to more rectangular ones at the top. Nothing is built perfectly straight and orderly—another decision to make our construction less easily recognizable from afar. The eye searches for simple patterns.

I admire how we disrupted the expected. Windows and doors spaced unevenly, not shaped in the same way. The courtyard behind me, used for sparring, is on the ground level, spacious and walled in to keep it hidden. The top of each wall is lined with walkways for guards. There are some always posted, set to protect our base.

On either side of the courtyard we cultivate vegetation, both edible and not. All life has purpose. The irrigation system put into place leaves room for beauty as well as practicality. Even apart from simple utility, it's good for morale. Good to see life can still exist, still grow, on Tajss.

The Devastation scoured the planet, killing too much. But even before those catastrophic wars, before that final death knell, Tajss was dying.

The planet we knew to be sentient was being overworked, its resources plundered at an alarming pace. When the First of the Order voiced their objections, it didn't simply fall on deaf ears. Oh no, nothing so benign as that.

In return for the warning that was already coming too late, the government and those in power launched a calculated smear campaign to malign the Order's name. It was a direct attempt to keep us at the fringes of society, and it worked. We were pushed aside, considered a cult with no value, brainwashed by stories without any basis in fact.

The attempt to save Tajss was a complete and utter failure. Money and power are not evil in and of themselves, but they certainly can fuel it. They can be a reason, an excuse to do the unthinkable, to remain shortsighted.

None of it matters now. Those who were in power have reaped the rewards of what they had sown. The planet was already desert before the war that decimated our society. The lush planet and varied biodomes were things of the distant past.

We still use some of our old technology here, an adapted version maintaining our crops and our security, but it's a mere sliver of what we used to have, nowhere near the level of what our cities once were.

So we are taught. The Order was pushed aside then. Now we must be ready. Ready to emerge and lead Tajss to a renaissance. One in tune with the planet itself, as we were before. Before the Devastation and before the corruption that shouted down and sidelined our founder.

Now I'm promoted. Years of work, all my hopes that had been aimed at this singular point in time, and it's hollow. Empty, meaningless, because never in a million years did I dream it would happen without Archion at my side.

I'd throw it all away to see him emerging from the desert, coming home. Frowning, I turn and watch the warriors sparring below. I barely see them though. What does any of this matter without my brother here to share it?

6

ASHLEE

The barren terrain slides by outside the rover window. I wonder if it's always been like this? Was Tajss always such a hellhole? The Zmaj don't recall, or if they do, they don't talk about it. The Devastation, as they call it, sounds terrible.

War always is, I guess, but I've only seen the idea in vids. My ancestors didn't leave Earth because of war. That was a thing of the past. They left because of overpopulation. Maybe that's a downfall of resolving war? Or, having resolved war, left us free to expand and explore?

Yeah, I like that better. Anything else is depressing and I prefer the good by far.

The rover is a godsend. I wish we had more of them available. This one, our only one, is held together by spit and duct tape as an engineer friend of mine used to say back on the ship. The terrain is deceptive—it looks smooth and beautiful but it's actually rough and tough. Where the sand is smooth the rover sinks and has to fight for its forward motion. Where it's not smoothed the rover has to climb over the strewn rocks and pockmarks, most of which are hidden by thin layers of the ever-blowing sand.

Luckily, we're fully prepared to be out here. We have enough rations, meteor glass, shock sticks, and epis to more than a make a roundtrip. Now we only have to come back victorious, and in one piece for that matter.

"Turn a little toward the right," Archion directs Nora.

"Copy that."

Nora is driving and Archion sits beside her in the copilot seat. He's been guiding her since he's the only one who knows where we're going. It makes us uncomfortably dependent on him, but he refused to draw a map or show us anything. I can't tell what he's guiding us by. I've been trying to spot any kind of landmark, anything that looks different, but each time he gives an order I see nothing that would indicate why he did.

I understand his need for complete secrecy, but it sure does make things inconvenient for the rest of us. If something happens to Archion, we're never making contact, or worse, surviving. I let that go. Some factors are just out of our control.

We're far enough away from the city now that the area around us is unfamiliar. Nora and I guzzle water, the incessant heat even in the rover wearing on us mercilessly. Archion, of course, appears largely unaffected. The Zmaj don't waste water through sweat no matter how hot they get. They're much better adapted to this ridiculously hot climate than we are, even with the epis to help us adjust.

"You want some jerky?" I ask Nora and Archion, pulling some out for myself.

It was marinated in Delilah's special sauce and then smoked. Not only does it hold up well, it's downright delicious. Perfect travel food.

"Sure," Nora agrees, holding out her hand for me to set a piece onto it. "Thank you."

Archion shakes his head when I offer him some.

"No, thank you."

I settle back into my seat and tear off a piece of the meat, chewing it slowly and thinking.

We've traveled far enough now I decide to bring some things up, see if I can pry out some answers to at least some of my questions.

"Nora, what do you think about Malcolm's dreams?" I ask idly. "Any idea what they may have been about?"

I'm questioning Nora but my attention is on Archion. His shoulders tense at my question. Interesting. I'm definitely on the right track.

"I don't know," Nora admits. "But I believe him." She looks over at Archion. "I saw Archion in a vision before I ever saw him in person. I didn't know what it meant even when he did appear." She shrugs. "I'm guessing that whatever Malcolm saw will make more sense once it actually happens."

"Maybe," I murmur, watching Archion carefully. "But that means the dreams or visions or whatever you want to call them aren't really all that useful."

Nora shakes her head and makes a sound at the back of her throat.

"I wouldn't say that. I knew Archion's appearance was significant when I saw him." She looks at him. "Not that I wouldn't have paid attention without a vision, but it was... a nice heads up, you know?"

"Maybe," I say, speaking slowly. "But Malcolm is so young. If he were a little older, maybe we could have picked his brain more. That might have helped."

"Perhaps we should stop and eat," Archion interjects, blinking rapidly and shifting in his seat.

I don't think it's a coincidence. His mood shifted as soon

as I started talking about Malcolm's dreams, but I don't push. I do take note, adding it to my mental collection. Trying to dive any deeper into the subject now won't help.

"Sure," Nora says, glancing at her mate. "Where to?"

"There, to the left. There should be a small oasis over that rise."

Nora obediently turns the rover in that direction. We drive over the sand dune he pointed out. I almost think he changed direction to interrupt the flow of conversation. That there won't be anything over the dune. I'm quickly proven wrong on that front.

As soon as we crest the dune, I see it. A small oasis. It's nothing to write home about, but it has enough trees and foliage to help beat the heat for a bit. Archion is obviously familiar with this area. A point in his favor, but also another piece of information to file away.

At the very least, it indicates he really is directing us somewhere that is familiar to him. I don't think the other Zmaj know any of the rest stops in this direction. Well, at least he's not just leading us out in a random direction to get away or run off with Nora. That was always a possibility.

Nora parks the car under the shade of a ridiculously tall —for Tajss—tree and we get out. Sighing, I arch my back to get the kinks out and walk to stretch my legs after the long drive. As the feeling slowly comes back to my butt, I watch Archion and Nora.

His eyes are hardly ever off her, even while he seems constantly on alert. Completely aware of his surroundings and any threat that may appear. He opens the back of the rover and takes out some of the provisions. Nora and I set up a little impromptu picnic, setting out more of the smoked jerky.

"It was about time to give the engine a break anyway," Nora notes. "This heat is hard on it."

"I can't think of anything worse than having it break down out here." I look around at the miles of nothingness all around us.

"You could say that again," Nora snorts.

The desert is a harsh place, even when not considering all the dangerous beasts that we could stumble across out here. The heat and scarcity of water alone is enough to do someone in. Best not to think too hard about that though. I'd never leave the city if I do. Well... if it meant leaving the lab, maybe I still would.

Archion remains silent, not sitting with Nora and me but remaining standing and silently chewing on his food. Nora and I continue to chat while we eat, but Archion isn't joining in. Is he still affected by the dream topic I brought up?

"How much farther is it?" I ask him.

He's the only one of us who would know.

"Not much farther," Archion answers, keeping it vague of course.

He stiffens, frowning, his tail rising behind him.

"What's wrong?" Nora asks.

Archion shakes his head, the frown deepening.

"Wait here," he orders.

Then he slips away.

My heart beats faster as adrenaline pumps through. Muscles quivering, breath shallow, and the hair on my arms standing on end. Shifting position to a crouch I'm ready to run for the rover but holding still as Archion ordered. Out here, not listening to a Zmaj will get you killed and I'm not stupid.

If this is a tactic to avoid conversation, it's going a little far. Nora and I exchange a worried glance in the wake of his quick departure. She's positioned herself similarly to me.

"What was that about?" I whisper.

She shakes her head, her eyes darting around and sweat running down her brow.

"I don't know," she whispers, looking at where Archion disappeared.

The lovely little picnic spot feels oddly exposed. Seconds tick past, counted off by the pounding of my heart. Afraid to even move, I bite my lip as my own sweat drips into my eyes, making them burn. Slowly I reach up and wipe it away when it starts to blur my vision.

I don't know how long we sit there, tense and waiting. Maybe ten minutes pass. Archion slips into view from behind one of the thick tree trunks, a tense look upon his face.

"Invaders are patrolling nearby," he explains, pitching his voice low so it won't carry. "It's best to take shelter before they see us."

Invaders? Shit. My heart was pounding, but now it's in overtime. My breasts hurt it's thrumming so hard and I don't dare to breathe. Eyes wide, I look around for a place to hide. Archion is good, really good, but he's not enough to take on a whole group of the hostile aliens. Nora and I aren't going to be much of an asset in a fight with the Invaders. They're too big and they're sure to have guns, while we only have shock sticks and Archion has his lochaber.

Neither Nora nor I argue. Grabbing our shock sticks from the rover we follow Archion, moving as silently as possible. The three of us move in a crouch, bent in half. It's uncomfortable as heck. My thighs burn and my lower back aches, but I grit my teeth and push past it.

Archion leads us to a nearby ridge covered with some foliage that I hope isn't one of the multiple types of plants on Tajss that will eat you. Damn, Tajss is tough. The foliage isn't pretty—red leaves that look like a kind of enlarged ivy—

which is a good sign that it's not dangerous. The prettiest things on Tajss are often the most deadly.

Archion drops onto his stomach and crawls along the ground up the ridge. The ground is sharp rock, cutting my hands and digging through my pants as I crawl across it. When we reach the top of the ridge Archion goes still and I mimic his action.

He scans the area below us. I'm too scared to take a breath, and my lungs burn until I exhale as slow as I can to avoid making any noise, then inhale. Archion is looking to the left. I strain my neck to try and see what he's looking at but I can't from my position.

He motions with one hand indicating we should follow. He shifts around, somehow managing to move his massive body through the foliage without causing any undue disturbance. It moves more as Nora and I pass under it than him. Another testament to his skill and training.

We run out of cover as make our way out of the small oasis. The hard, sharp ground softens until we're on the sand again. A break in the ground suddenly appears in front of me, dropping into a shadowed crevasse. It's dark and relatively cool inside the small space.

Archion takes Nora's hand and a moment later he lowers her into it. Our eyes meet as her head drops below the edge. She gives me a reassuring smile, but my stomach clamps tight and a cold sweat covers my back.

When Archion turns to me I stare at him wide-eyed. I can't do this. No. I can't go into that tight, small space. I'll take my chances out here.

He frowns and motions insistently, grabbing for my hand. I jerk it away and he hisses. Shaking my head violently side to side I crawl backward. He grabs for me again and this time he's too fast. He clamps down on my forearm with a vise-like strength. I struggle but can't break his grip.

"No, no, no." I have enough presence of mind not to scream, but fear is rising faster and faster.

Scrabbling my feet and grasping with my free hand, I try to stop his inexorable pull forward. It doesn't do me any good. I can't break free.

I know I'm being stupid but I'm watching myself react and I can't stop it. My heart is in my throat, I can't breathe, and my vision blurs as he lowers me into the crack in the ground.

I immediately feel trapped and I freeze. I want to move. Want to scream. Want to claw my way free, but I can't. The rock walls are so close I can't take a full breath. Sweat pours down my body, soaking the cloth of my clothes. I'm going to die.

Panting, I manage to turn my head and see the opening. The bright, open space calls to me, but it's on the other side of Nora. If I could push past her I could be free!

I go for it. Sliding toward her, trying to force her out of my way.

"Ashlee," she hisses, digging her feet into the ground and not moving.

Damn it, move!

"Ashlee," she whispers more insistent.

She grabs my face between her hands, forcing me to look at her. Tears are streaming down my face, I'm panting, I can't do this.

Archion drops into the crevasse on the other side of her. His massive form makes it worse, blocking out the light and my vision of the free, open space.

"Please," I beg her, shaking, unable to control myself.

Archion glances toward me, a deep frown on his face, and he hisses, shaking his head. He pulls a knife out, gripping the hilt tightly. There's a moment I'm certain he's going to cut my throat to shut me up. It's the only thing that breaks my panic.

Nora runs her hands over my face, staring at me, wiping the sweat away from my eyes. I take a shaky breath, close my eyes, and focus on another breath. I'm okay. Stupid, but okay. Nora kisses my forehead.

"It's okay," she whispers.

I bite off any response and hold my breath when I hear the approaching sound of footsteps. We all go completely still. Maybe they won't come here. Maybe they'll pass us by and we'll have a cool, close-call story to tell everyone when we get back. Maybe—

A figure blocks the light from the opening. It's silhouetted against the sunlight, so I can't make out specific features, though I know from past experience that textured blue skin covers that elongated head. The full black eyes with no whites to them blink into the shadows where we're hiding, thick brow ridges shadowing them even more.

The lipless mouth filled with sharp teeth is bracketed by tusks curving out and around until they almost touch in the front. The Invader has six arms in total, three on either side with the middle appendages being the largest and most functional. Those end in three-fingered hands with only one joint, black claws tipping the ends. The other four arms are smaller and thinner, ending in small pincers proportional in size. Everything but the head, hands, and feet is covered by a matte brown carapace-like armor with an emblem sewed onto the left part of the chest: a yellow pincer on a brown background.

Some of this I see, some my mind fills in from what I know to be there. I can't see everything with the bright suns in the background, but I don't have to.

The Invaders are a familiar threat by this point, seemingly ready to attack us ceaselessly. There's no rhyme or reason to their attacks. No one knows why or when but they do seem to be after the meteorite glass. It's not clear why they're here but there may very well be something deeper going on. Prior to them it was the Zzlo. They were a familiar threat, to the Zmaj at least. Space pirates who make a living in the slave trade or scavenging. They were the ones who attacked our generation ship and caused the wreck. All of this crosses my mind in a split second.

The alien presence appears and Archion moves so fast if I blinked I'd have missed it. He has the thing in a headlock, dragging it into the crevasse with us and slicing its throat wide open with his knife.

I gasp at the swift violence but muffle the sound with a hand over my mouth as I press farther back into the tight space while trying to avoid the warm fluid spraying in a wide arc from the Invader.

The Invader struggles in Archion's arms to no avail, and it doesn't take long for it to bleed out. As it goes limp in his arms, Archion drops it but it must have been faking. It lets out a staccato roar alerting the rest of its group before it stills.

No bueno. Archion barely spares us a glance before he steps out of the relative safety of the shelter. What is he doing? At least those things can only enter here one at a time.

Nora and I look at each other. She has her shock stick ready, but I lost mine in the grips of my panic. She slides closer to the entrance.

"No," I whisper, "stay back."

Her shoulders tense and silent she shakes her head. She slides forward. Straining my senses, I try to figure out what's happening. If anything happens to Archion, we're screwed. Nora ignores me, continuing to inch her way toward the opening.

I hear the distinct sound of Archion's lochaber whistling

through the air and then the roar of his opponents, quick footsteps, and the sound of flesh hitting flesh. It's a confused cacophony of sounds, overlapping and layered, followed by a heavy silence.

Between one beat and the next, the sound is all just...gone. Followed by a horrible, unnerving stillness. What happened?

I can't hear any small sounds beyond my own breathing and the pounding of my heart in my ears. Did Archion defeat the Invaders? Or are they going to rush inside and overtake us now that Archion is...

I jerk as a shadow blocks the sunlight once more. This time, it's by a different figure altogether.

"We cannot linger. They are only the first line of eyes. Quickly—we must hurry past another group in that loud machine while we still can."

I snap my open mouth closed and nod at the commanding words. Nora and I scramble out, blinking at the abrupt change of light. I keep moving, almost blindly, hoping I'm going in the right direction. I trip over something and stumble, squinting, trying to see, only to realize it is a body.

Swallowing bile, I tear my eyes away and try not to look down. My brain takes a snapshot of the carnage of its own accord. Gritting my teeth, I keep going, following the others back around the dune to where we can climb up to the small picnic area right where we left it.

I grab my water skin, but we leave behind the scraps of meat and fruit. There isn't time as we pile into the rover. As soon as all of us are in, Nora starts the vehicle and punches the accelerator. Archion's right. It isn't silent, but if we keep moving, it should hopefully be okay.

I'd rather be in the rover than back inside that small ridge. My cheeks flush hot, embarrassment flooding through at my reaction. It was completely irrational and stupid, but there was no controlling it.

"I'm sorry," I say, forcing the words past the thick lump in my throat.

Archion looks over his shoulder, hard eyes staring judgmentally, and the sick feeling in my stomach grows worse. I can't keep meeting his eyes. Dropping mine, I stare at the floor.

"It's fine," Nora says, not looking back.

"It's... not." I try to say more but I can't speak.

"Each of has our own monsters to fight," Archion says. "You did not give in. There is nothing to be ashamed of in fighting what's inside of you."

His words draw me out and I meet his eyes, looking for any sign of bullshit. If it's there, I can't see it. He's sincere and the most open I've seen him... ever. Thoughtfully, I nod. Nora smiles at him but keeps most of her attention on what's in front of us.

"Right," I swallow.

Leaning back in the seat I close my eyes and let my thoughts drift. Unfortunately images of the Invaders strewn about hit me once more with brutal detail. Cut-up bodies, some of them dismembered, limbs broken at odd angles. I know I saw a head separated from the rest of its body...

Stop it.

There's no use dwelling over something that couldn't be avoided. If Archion didn't kill those Invaders, they would have killed or enslaved us. Neither is an acceptable option. I try to switch gears, try to glean information from what I saw. Try to think objectively.

Okay.

Archion took down a group of Invaders by himself. Quickly and expertly. This is another clear example of how fast and skilled Archion is. I've never seen another Zmaj move as fast as he did to slice that first Invader's throat. Nor could any of the others I know take down four Invaders at once.

Not this quickly anyway, and not without taking some damage. The other Zmaj are still impressive fighters, that's not up for debate, but before Archion showed up... I didn't even know there *was* another level.

Opening my eyes, I stare at Archion's hard profile. He is scanning through the front windscreen, ever vigilant. We're lucky he was with us. I wince as Nora steps down harder on the accelerator and the engine roars in response.

Now that Archion mentioned the loudness of the engine, I can't help but notice it even more, but there is no help for it. We're moving much faster in the vehicle. And if Archion didn't think speed was of the essence, he wouldn't have suggested it. So I hold onto the seat and hope we make it.

7

KHAL

*a*n alarm blares and my eyes snap open, my training taking over before I am fully awake.

I'm out of my pallet before the reverberation of the loud gong finishes sounding the third and final time. Grabbing my lochaber and my knives that hang near the door for just this reason, I race out of my quarters and down the stairs.

My post is some distance from the Order's home, but I'm fast, my feet barely touching the ground as I move with a practiced speed to reach it swiftly.

Staying low as I reach the high ground, I push into the sand and obscure myself with it before turning my attention to scanning the desert. The rush of adrenaline flows through me, heightening my senses.

Combined with my particular training, I take in the scene and process it quickly. Something glints, reflecting the light of the moon. I don't know what is causing it but it's moving, and fast. Closing my protective lenses I watch, carefully judging its approach. It's coming closer, right toward my post.

The glint becomes a dark blob which resolves into a boxy

shape. A loud roar echoes over the sands to me, obviously some form of engine propelling the thing. Whoever or whatever is guiding it seems to know exactly where they're going. That's not good.

The real question is—who is inside that metal box? And why are they on the edge of our territory? There is nothing else on this path but us, a deliberate choice on the Order's part. Chance encounters are rare to nonexistent.

As I watch, trying to glean anything else from its appearance, the vehicle stops. And then the occupants get out. My breath catches in my chest at the sight of a tall, familiar figure. One I would know anywhere.

Archion.

So taken am I by the sight of my brother that I don't register the two figures with him until an instant later, when I hear a higher-pitched voice.

Tearing my eyes away from Archion's obviously hale and healthy form, I take in the others. Whoever they are, they're clearly not native to Tajss and just as obviously female. Incredible!

Small and curved, with paler skin that looks infinitely softer than ours, I cannot help but stare. The Leader has long claimed he had a vision of strangers falling from the stars. Seers of the Council have had visions of strangers crashing on Tajss. But, as is the way with visions, we had not seen it with our eyes.

None of the Order has seen sign of a ship, nor of the strangers themselves. Until now.

All of this goes runs through my mind while I stare, even as my attention inexorably shifts to that of the emerald-eyed female. There is something about her that draws my attention more than her counterpart, a magnetism. She pulls on something deep in my core. It's a draw that I immediately resent.

It creates an odd combination coupling with the relief of finding my brother. Archion is alive. He isn't maimed in any way, no sign of injury I can see, but... he has also brought outsiders with him.

Confusing matters more, the outsiders are females. Perhaps the Council will not frown too deeply on this for that reason, but I cannot be certain. It's much too early to tell how they will react. I draw in a deep breath, scouting the area for danger before sliding out of the sand.

I catch the scent of bitter blood when the wind shifts and my eye goes to my brother. I recognize the familiar scent of the alien blood. Those aliens have been a problem to us, Archion and I have previously hunted them. That he is unharmed but carries the scent of their blood is a testament. He is a phenomenal warrior.

My smile is so wide my cheeks hurt. I wonder how many of the Invaders he killed this time. How many fell under the expert swing of his lochaber?

Straightening to my full height as I rise out of the sand, I start down the dune toward the small group. I am happy the alarm brought me this, but the situation is also more complicated than I could have ever expected.

Archion sees me and a smile crosses his face before he bursts into a run to intercept me.

"Brother!" he cries out, pulling me into a hard embrace.

Closing my eyes I take a deep breath of his scent, crushing him against me as a wash of sweet relief hits me. He is alive. I feel something inside me shift back to where it should be, my world once again returning to the correct order.

"I worried when you did not return," I inform him in a low voice.

"I am sorry to have worried you so," he returns, pulling

back so he can meet my eyes. "I returned as soon as it was possible."

I nod then look past him to the females watching us.

"It seems as though much has happened while you were gone," I remark pointedly.

He nods, his face turning more serious.

"Yes. It is why I was gone for so long." He turns to the female with straight brown hair. "Khal, this is my mate, Nora." Mates? I nod at her even as the word sends a shockwave through me. "And this is Ashlee. She has joined us in a diplomatic capacity, as a representative for her people."

I nod to the emerald-eyed female as well, taking in her shining, light brown hair and beautiful face. Large eyes with long lashes, a delicate nose, soft pink mouth. Her body is small and delicate as well, though curved in places I find... pleasing.

I have to force my gaze away when Archion continues to talk, too distracted at the sight of this Ashlee.

"I discovered potential allies, a group—a society—consisting of others like Nora as well as other Zmaj. And possible resources."

"I see," I murmur, my response neutral.

I do not know quite what to say. When I imagined Archion returning, it was not like... this. He searches my face.

"Once they are settled, I will seek the audience of the Council."

I take a deep breath.

"They think you must be dead," I say bluntly.

He must know. I do not want him to walk in blindly. Archion's smile falters, a flicker of doubt crossing his eyes as the meaning of my words clearly registers. The Council has decided he was lost. They may not welcome him back now. Especially with outsiders in tow.

It is a great violation of our rules to bring anyone not of

the Order back to our home. A violation that cannot be over-looked or ignored, so embedded is it in the structure of our society, rooted as it is in our safety and the safety of that which we are to protect. Archion understands all of this.

He has played a key role in the Order for so long now, knowing exactly what is acceptable and what is not. Yet...here is, in complete violation of those very laws. I see his determination to push past all of this, to reach the goal he has in mind, and I trust in his sheer force of will. Still I do not know if it will be enough in this instance.

"They will understand once I speak to them," he says in a low voice.

I nod slowly, locking eyes with him. I hope he is right.

8

ASHLEE

I didn't know what to expect when I saw the tall, muscled Zmaj warrior in that flowing sand-colored robe. His handsome face is unreadable as he looks us over with intense, piercing purple-blue eyes. His eyes match the pale blue iridescence of the scales I could see, his dark hair windblown and yet still framing the hard contours of his face perfectly.

Yeah, my heart skipped a beat. But who could blame me?

His eyes, the coloring of his scales, the flexing muscles of the unfamiliar Zmaj, I didn't even realize the familial resemblance until Archion drew him into a tight hug. Brother. They called each other brother. The similarity in their faces tells me it isn't just a title they share between any member of their group, but an actual genetic tie.

Though I don't take the heartfelt reunion to mean that we're out of the fire with their secretive group. In fact, from the warning look on Khal's face and his loaded words, it doesn't sound like Archion is going to receive the world's warmest welcome.

I share a look with Nora as we follow Archion's even

more mysterious brother, leaving the rover behind. I hope it's still there if we need it.

Khal stops in front of...nothing. Just another patch of sand. He gives us a sharp look as he crouches down with purpose.

"I am trusting that you are not here with ill intentions. This entrance is meant to remain hidden from outsiders."

He doesn't wait for us to answer before he opens a latch I was not even able to see, drawing back a thick door, sand pouring off of it and revealing steps leading down into the darkness. He doesn't hesitate, disappearing down them without another word. Archion looks back at us.

"Follow closely. The tunnel is not long. I will come in after you."

All right then. Time to go into that dark underground tunnel with a dangerous stranger I don't know. Perfect. Seems like a good idea.

Cold chills race up and down my arms and legs as I look into that yawning black pit of despair. Sure, I know rationally that it's nothing of the sort. It's a tunnel. Right, fine. Unfortunately, rational and my irrational fear aren't on speaking terms.

Nora places a hand on my shoulder, squeezing me reassuringly. Closing my eyes, I focus on my breath. In and out, in and out. I'm an idiot, this is stupid, it's irrational. There's nothing to fear.

Taking a deep breath, I follow him down into the darkness, hoping I'm not making a mistake. I step down carefully, feeling with my feet as I go, not opening my eyes, letting Nora's firm grip guide me.

When we're at the bottom I open my eyes and let them adjust, trying my best to not give in to the clamoring fears assaulting every one of my senses. As my eyes adjust, I realize it's actually not that dark down here.

Sporadic torches light the way, casting enough light that there is no risk of accidentally tripping. The tunnel itself is well maintained, the ground smooth and clear, the walls straight. It's obviously not a naturally occurring construction or one of the massive, round tunnels left behind by the roaming zemlja. Which begs the question, how do they keep one of them from plowing through it?

No, no, no. Stupid thought, don't think it, Ashlee. Panic rises, my throat closes, and I'm gasping and trying to desperately catch my breath.

"It's okay," Nora says, encouragingly. "We're fine. Nothing's going to happen to you."

The new Zmaj looks over his shoulder, his purple eyes catching the light in such a way that they look like burning pools of lavender. They burn into me, digging under my skin, finding me beneath all my facades and seeing the true me in some strange, metaphysical way that I'd never believe if I weren't experiencing it.

A connection happens between us. A spark—it's a moment that sears its way into the depths of who I am. The panic recedes before it's leaving an empty calm behind it. My breathing eases, my heart slows, and I nod. He returns the gesture before turning and resuming leading us on.

We only walk for maybe ten minutes before the tunnel turns and he glides up another set of steps. I hear the distinctive sound of him pushing open another door, but I don't hurry forward. I hang back, not wanting to be the one to follow directly after. I don't want to be that close to him, not yet. My nerves are thrumming with so much more than the panic I was experiencing. I don't know what I'm feeling or thinking but if I were to accidentally brush against him….

Nora stops next to me and waits too, looking me over with obvious concern. I give her a wan smile, feeling shaky and uncertain. It's not a feeling I recall ever having had before. Archion moves past us.

"Follow closely," he murmurs.

The stairs are as steep as the first ones we countered, but this time the door opens up into a small room rather than the desert. I blink at the brighter torchlight illuminating the ten-by-ten-foot square space.

The floor is softened with animal skins tossed haphazardly around. A low, sleek table with some earthenware dishes on it sits to one side surrounded by thick cushions rather than chairs. Colorful tapestries adorn the walls along with small bits of decorations incorporating beads and feathers. The walls themselves are the same color as the sand outside.

Moving over to the single window I look out and can see it blends into the surroundings. I frown as I look around. Unless...

Is this part of the surroundings? Is it carved out of a rock face? I look around more carefully, noting how smooth the walls are. If that's the case, it's pretty damn impressive. And the room is a perfect square. That takes a good amount of skill. Skill and patience. It looks like the Tribe could learn a thing or two from the Order about construction.

When I turn back around Khal is gone.

"Where did he go?" I wonder out loud.

Archion crosses his arms over his chest but doesn't speak.

"I think he'll be right back," Nora says.

He returns on the heels of her statement with four armed Zmaj in robes similar to his own. They don't look like they're the welcoming committee. Nora takes a step forward when they surround Archion, but I lay a hand on her arm to hold her back.

She looks over at me with frustration, but I shake my head slightly. Fighting against this will only make things worse right now, for us and for Archion. I'm almost positive I'm reading this right and if outsiders are defending me it won't look good for him. Presenting ourselves as physical threats won't help us either.

She holds my gaze for a beat, then two, clearly fighting her protective instincts. At last she nods sharply and stays put. Her arm doesn't relax under my hand, however. Not that I blame her. I have no idea what they're going to do to him.

"I will see you soon," Archion reassures Nora, his demeanor completely calm.

As though he was expecting this. Would have been nice to be given a heads up. Nora nods.

"You better," she mutters.

He smiles at her, a glimmer of humor reaching his serious eyes, then he nods. And that's the only time the guards give the two of them.

Archion disappears through a door with his armed escort at alert, though he clearly has no intention of fighting. And we're left alone with his brother.

I turn my attention back to the other Zmaj, only to see him setting out food and water on some kind of ceramic cups and plates on that short table. This clearly was no surprise to him either. Though I guess he was the one to call the guards over.

"Eat. Drink. The desert is harsh," he orders gruffly, his eyes flitting over us.

"Thank you," I murmur.

His eyes briefly meet my own, the intensity in them making my breath catch once more. It's like he's running on a totally different level. He barely nods, then leaves through the same door they led Archion through without another word.

"Great," Nora mutters, lowering herself down onto one of the cushions surrounding the table. "Off to a stellar start."

I can't argue with the anxiety in her voice. Our only ally here has been taken into custody. We have no idea what this outpost even looks like. And it isn't clear that they'll let us go no matter what the outcome of Archion's meeting is. These warriors obviously don't play around with their secrets.

If Archion's request is rejected, I'm sure that we won't even learn the reason why. I'm also sure that if they let us go, the door to the tunnel we used to come in here will vanish like it was never there. Though all of this cloak-and-dagger stuff does beg the question—why go to so much trouble hiding if there isn't something to hide?

I don't say any of that out loud. It won't help Nora get through this, so I keep my thoughts to myself. Lowering myself onto the surprisingly fluffy cushion next to Nora I wrap my arm around the dejected woman.

"Eat something. It'll make you feel better."

She shakes her head, turning her face away from the table.

"I can't. It's too hot—even looking at food is making me nauseous."

My hand stills for a moment on her back, but then I continue rubbing. It actually isn't all that hot in here, and the journey through the desert wasn't that bad. Nora isn't a particularly delicate person either.

I don't say anything, but I know in my gut that there aren't only two of us in this room. She's pregnant. I have no doubt about it. It's not my place to say it though, especially under these circumstances. Nora and Archion will figure it out soon enough.

Heck, maybe this kid will come out levitating. So many odd, arcane-tinged events have happened recently that I am fully ready to suspend disbelief. This planet may very well be mystical in nature after all.

"Well, why don't we think about something else? There's

no point in worrying over something that we can't change. How are you liking the city?"

Nora seemed happy enough with the Tribe until Archion came along. Then the Tribe elders had an issue with Archion's refusal to divulge details of his past, specifically information about the Order. Experiencing this place, I can see why he's such a closed book. Seems like the way to be here. Nora shrugs, taking a deep breath.

"It's fine," she murmurs. "I like how much closer the Tribe is though," she admits. "Everyone in the city is much more scattered, less linked together, you know?"

"I know what you mean," I agree. "That happens with a larger space, but that doesn't mean there isn't a community. Especially now with the babies and children—everyone has come together to raise the next generation. It really does take a village. Although, I guess in this case it takes a city."

Nora chuckles, shaking her head. Taking the sweating pitcher in her hand, she pours some water for herself. I wonder how they have such cold water here? Bringing the cup up to her pale lips, she takes a careful sip. I watch her discreetly, noting her color. If she gets any worse, I might have to say something after all. She sighs, lowering the cup.

"Yeah, I suppose so. At this point, I'm fine with living wherever as long as I'm with Archion." She looks over at me, her smile wan. "What a sap, huh?"

"No, you just sound like someone who's found her mate," I push back. "Look at the bright side here—we don't have vids anymore or many books to read. Luckily." I lean toward her, raising an index finger for emphasis. "Our lives aren't boring, or we'd all be climbing the walls by now."

That surprises a laugh out of her, color flushing her face. Good.

"Yeah, I guess so. Though sometimes I do look at back on

the ridiculously long days on the ship and miss it. Miss the sameness, the monotony. The safety."

"Sure. But there was no Archion on that ship," I point out.

"True," she sighs, shaking her head. "I'm lucky I found him. But it sure does seem like our road is a lot harder than anyone else's mating has been so far."

I nod. She's not wrong about that.

I start to move on to a different subject to distract her when Khal's face flashes across my mind's eye. I immediately push it away. I'm here on a diplomatic mission. Stay focused on that.

No matter how hunky I find any of the players.

9

KHAL

$\mathcal{I}$ stand outside the inner sanctum. Perhaps I should not be here, but that is why I deliberately did not ask Tashak for permission. I have to know what is happening in there, need to know what reception my brother is receiving.

However, hours of waiting later, even my brain it is beginning to shut down from the endless rounds of questioning and I'm not the target.

I can hear every word through the closed door, but even if I was not able to, I would know exactly what was being said at this point. Tashak has droned on for so long, asking the same questions over and over again as if expecting a different answer. Simply listening to the questioning is tiring.

I don't know how my brother continues to answer so methodically. I shift my feet as I hear Archion reply once more. His voice is calm as he answers the question for what must be the hundredth time, but I know that he worries about the females he brought with him.

Especially his mate, Nora. He must know that they are

safe, that I would not allow harm to come to them, but I know that he still wants to be there with them. I can hear it in the slight tinge of impatience that is beginning to enter his voice.

"Why did you break protocols? You and I both know you know them as well as anyone, as well as any Councilor."

Tashak's voice is as hard as it was when the interview started. Perhaps even more so. He is clearly not content with the answers he has received thus far. Though I do not know why he believes they will change.

"The circumstances were unusual," Archion explains once more. "Not only did I find people that we have not encountered before, I found females—surely you can understand why I would stay to gather information."

Archion's voice is straining, his calm façade wearing thin.

"Gathering information I understand. However, you have obviously done much more than that," Tashak's voice whips out. Archion remains silent, clearly unable to refute that claim. "You should not have engaged with the ones you found," Tashak continues in that unbending voice. "Outsiders are not welcome in the Order's territory. And there is very good reason for that. You know this."

"Again, I understand. But we cannot be so rigid! I understand I broke protocol—"

"I do not think you understand to quite what degree you have broken protocol!" Tashak interrupts, raising his voice in ire. "To what degree you have broken the words that we vow to live by here! And you have still not given me a sufficient answer as to why. Why did you do so? What possible draw could have been so strong that you broke the code of conduct in such a bold and unthinking manner?"

A heavy pause, the silence even louder after the intensity Tashak's voice. Archion's response is careful, just as all of his words have been thus far.

"As I have said before, the Zmaj and the humans that I encountered needed help. I drew the Invaders over to their group—it was only right for me to stay and protect them. I understand that I should not have engaged. But I could not stand back and do nothing, watching them fight for their lives when I could help..."

I listen to Archion answer, frowning. There is something not quite right about his answers. I have been thinking about it for a while, but could not quite put my finger on why until now. Rather than direct, to the point, and succinct, his answers are long and winding. Almost as if he is avoiding some particular point, his words dancing around a secret. It's not like him.

In fact, it is a very strange thing for my brother to do. He has always been straightforward, known for following every word of protocol, for being a stellar example of an Order warrior. This Archion... I almost do not recognize him.

"...we should at least attempt to have a dialogue with them, talk about the possibility of trading and working together. I would not have risked so much if I did not think these newcomers had much to offer the Order. It does not make any sense to not at least see if we could develop a partnership. A relationship that could be mutually beneficial."

It seems as though Archion is done answering questions. His words are utterly sincere as he pushes Tashak.

"I see that I have very much underestimated your understanding of what the Order is," Tashak returns coldly. "The entire point of our existence, our sole purpose, is to protect Tajss, to protect its secrets. That is our number one priority and will remain so no matter what impression you have of these newcomers. Until such time that we can confidently ascertain the true nature and motives of these people, they cannot be welcomed into Order territory. Not if we are to fulfill our first and only real directive." He sighs and I can imagine him shaking his head in disappointment. "I do not understand why you cannot grasp this simple notion. Why you have let your emotions cloud your judgment in such a severe matter as to bring possible threats to the heart of the Order's sanctuary."

"I have explained myself quite thoroughly," Archion starts, the irritation stronger in his tone now. "But you refuse to listen..."

I wince as the interview quickly becomes heated between the two.

Should I go inside? I want to be there, want to be by Archion's side to support him. I understand some of the points that he is making even if they do disagree with the protocol. I do not know if I would have made the same decisions, but I do not think that Archion's intent was to call the Order's leadership into question. I shift toward the door but stop myself.

I am duty bound not to interfere. This is the Councilor's purview. It is up to him what happens. My interference will not be looked upon positively. Perhaps if I—

"...if you just open up your mind briefly to the idea that they have something to offer—"

The growl I hear in Archion's voice stills me. Clear aggression will not be tolerated, especially in this circumstance.

"Enough!" Tashak explodes, interrupting Archion's continued attempt at persuasion. "I am ordering the females out of our territory! They do not belong here. They should not be here. Perhaps I was wrong about you. Perhaps your judgment can no longer to be trusted. Be that as it may, I still have a responsibility to the Order even if you do not feel the same."

This is not good. Even after my brief interaction with Archion, I know he will not appreciate the females being kicked out. He will not be separated from them, especially Nora. I hesitate no longer.

Shoving the door open, I step inside, ready to stop Archion from losing his temper and possibly making matters even worse for both himself and for the females. I take in the room quickly, the familiar carving on the walls and the bits and pieces of machinery glowing in corners of the room.

I note the four guards, two by the door that I just burst through, and another two posted at the other door across from me. They are all focused upon Archion until I burst in, but I ignore them in favor of Archion and Tashak.

They do not look away from each other as I hurry in, locked in an intense stare. It's an odd picture. Archion without his robe, Tashak in the jewel tones of a Councilor. Both a symbol of where they are in that moment. Both of their jaws are clenched, Archion's fists closed tightly at his sides as he stares at Tashak. The Councilor doesn't look away when he speaks.

"Khal, take the females back to their transport. You are to watch them until they have left the Order's territory."

The words are firm, final. Unshaking.

Archion's nose flares in response, his jaw clenched so tightly his temples turn white. He turns his gaze on to me, his golden eyes incandescent with emotion. His mate is being told to leave. Tashak wants to separate him from his other half.

It's unreal. I can't believe the words. Every Zmaj knows that a mate is for eternity. How could Tashak do this?

I see the same thoughts run across Archion's face, even though he says nothing, his eyes speaking for him. I do not want to do this. Despite the protocol, it feels wrong. Feels wrong to do to anybody, let alone my brother, my hero. If I don't do it, Tashak will send someone else to carry the order through.

I don't trust anyone more than I trust myself with the safety of Archion's mate. I'm torn between duty, loyalty, and emotion, but I know what must be done. And I must do it for all of our sakes.

Nodding sharply, I turn and walk through the same doors I entered by. I hope my brother can forgive me.

10

ASHLEE

*W*e wait for hours.

Eventually Nora starts nibbling on food while we wait, her face pensive. Sighing, I get up from where I'm lying down on the cushions. Nora looks up when I stand.

"What are you doing?" she asks, watching me move toward the door that they led Archion through.

"Just checking," I murmur, my hand closing over the cool handle of the door.

Maybe there isn't anyone posted there now. Maybe they're all busy with Archion. It's worth a shot anyway. Taking a deep breath, I open the door and step through, figuring I may as well look confident in the hopes of faking my way out.

A Zmaj in sand-colored robes steps in front of me, blocking my path. I let out a silent half breath, my heart jumping in my chest, and look up at his impassive face. He doesn't look at all impressed with my confidence.

"Okay," I murmur as he glares at me silently. "I'll just..."

I gesture toward the open door and back up until I'm

through it. He watches me with that same intensity until I close the door on his face.

"Very productive," Nora mutters from behind me.

I shrug, turning back around as my heart starts to calm.

"At least we know for sure now that we can't leave."

That doesn't sound very comforting. I sit back down next to Nora, sinking back into my thoughts. We ran out of things to say a while back, and Nora doesn't seem like she wants to enter into more small talk. I understand. That's her mate out there. And we have no idea what they're doing with him. So we sit and wait. And wait some more.

I'm starting to wonder if we're going to have to go to sleep without getting any word back when that same door I tried to go through opens and Archion's brother walks in.

I quickly rise to my feet, Nora doing the same as he takes both of us in.

"Where is Archion?" Nora demands, craning her head to look behind him.

His lips tighten, but he doesn't answer Nora's question.

"I will escort you back to your vehicle," he says instead.

It isn't a question.

"What?" I ask, my mind racing.

"You're kicking us out without Archion? Where is my mate?" Nora steps forward, her voice rising.

I grab ahold of her arm, keeping her back. I don't want her to get physical. I'm not sure what the reaction will be.

"Let me go!" she orders, trying to twist out of my grip. "Where the hell is Archion? What is going to be done with him? I'm not leaving without him!"

I grab both of Nora's arms and forcibly turn her toward me, careful to be gentle but firm. It's a struggle. She isn't a weak woman.

"Nora!" I say sharply, trying to cut through the hysteria

trying to take hold of her. "Nora, calm down. We need to get to the bottom of this. This isn't helping."

Nora's eyes slowly focus on me, her face pale. She clamps her lips shut and nods her head sharply. I don't fully trust her in this moment, so I keep a hold on her and then turn my head to look at Archion's brother.

"Look, what's your name? Did I catch it right out there, Khal? You're his brother, right? And a Zmaj, you all can't be that different from the ones we know. How could any of you consider separating mates?"

"I am Khal," he says, standing stiff, his mouth barely opening with the words, but I don't miss the tension in his shoulders or the way his eyes narrow.

"Can we talk to someone? Whoever's in charge?" I ask. "You can't expect Archion's mate to leave him here."

He shakes his head. "No, you must leave. If you fight, I will have to force the issue. And I do not want—"

Nora jerks out of my hold. I turn toward her, ready to catch her again if she is going to try to attack, but she doesn't have any intention of attacking anyone.

Doubling over, she projectile vomits all over the floor, covering the animal skins with the splatter. Silence reigns in the room, punctuated only by Nora's labored breathing. The Zmaj stops moving toward us, staring at the mess on the floor and then at Nora for a long moment. Ignoring him I rush over to help pull her away from the mess and set her down on a clean cushion. Tears are streaming down her face as she collapses.

"Shhh. Here, have this," I urge, handing her a cup of water as I rub her back. "You'll feel better."

"I'm not going to feel better anytime soon," she says around her quiet sobs.

I feel my heart crack for her.

"Is she sick?" Khal demands.

I turn to glare at him.

"No, she isn't sick," I bite out. "She's pregnant, you know, with child? God, are all of you so damn blind? And let's be clear about this, it's Archion's child. I know you've already figured that out so don't act like a douche-waffle."

His eyes widen and his cheeks pale. He stares at Nora, obviously stunned.

"I... will return," he mutters.

He whirls around and disappears through the door. It's obvious he's going to inform whoever is in charge. Great. I think.

I turn back to Nora, wrapping my arms around her.

"Pregnant?" she whispers.

I squeeze.

"Yeah. I'm sorry. I didn't mean to just yell that out in front of you like that."

She shakes her head.

"Extenuating circumstances," she murmurs. "Pregnant," she repeats, awe clear in her voice. She covers her stomach with her hand. "Archion's baby," she says in wonder.

I hold her, staying silent as she has this moment to let it settle in. The door is firmly shut once more. I hope this changes their reactions. That they won't be so cruel as to force us to leave now that they know Nora is carrying one of their own's baby. But...I don't know.

If they were willing to shove Archion's mate out, would they be willing to shove his pregnant mate out as well?

11

KHAL

*B*lood thrums in my ears as I run out of the room which holds the two females. The guards drop their lochabers in surprise but I'm past them before they bring them to bear. I don't have time to explain.

A child?

I cannot even firmly wrap my mind around the idea. A child...

A... future. What does this mean? What will this change? Will it change anything? How could it not?

A storm of emotions assails my stoic training, colliding so that I can't single one out as I rush toward the Councilor's chamber. There is no time for me to wrestle with my own feelings. I must report this news as soon as possible. This time, I don't linger outside the door or even bother knocking.

This news will not allow me to do so. Bursting directly through the door, I rush inside. The two guards on either side of the door attempt to stop me, but I will not be deterred from my goal.

I duck under their grasping arms and move past one only to dodge another blow from the other.

I do not want to hurt anyone, but I can't let them stop me. I punch the closest one in the stomach hard enough he bends over, gasping for breath. No real damage but it keeps him from stopping me.

The other guard growls and rushes. The bijass rises, red rage fueling itself on the storm of uncertainty from the news I carry. Straightening, I fall into a ready stance, prepared to fight him as well.

"Enough! Stand down!"

The guard stumbles to a halt at Tashak's commanding voice, though I can see he doesn't want to. I watch him warily, not trusting that he won't try something anyway.

"Khal, what is the meaning of this?" Tashak demands.

Deciding the guard is not going to attack me now, I carefully turn my head to meet the Councilor's eyes.

"One of the females, Nora. She's pregnant...with Archion's child."

I could deliver this with more tact or decorum, but I'm struggling with the bijass and my own whirling thoughts. Being diplomatic or following decorum are the last things on my mind.

Tashak stares wide-eyed, his face going slack and losing the irritable, harsh expression that was there even when I left on his orders. I understand the reaction. I don't think I'm out of it yet. The shock of it is too great, the reaction too bone-deep. To Tashak's credit, he recovers faster than I would have expected.

"What?" Archion exclaims.

My brother is as surprised as the rest of us. His mouth hangs open, his tail shifts nervously back and forth. He starts toward me when Tashak turns on him.

"Did you know this? Were you aware of her...condition...before you brought her here? Could you really be this reckless? Is it, indeed, your child?" He rubs at his face. "Has your judgment suffered even more than I fear?"

Archion's eyes narrow, his hands balling into his face. Every muscle tenses, his wings rustle, and his tail all but vibrates with the tension. His hard eyes lock onto Tashak with murderous intent.

Careful, brother. I watch closely as he barely controls his rage. When he speaks, his words are tightly controlled, devoid of any apparent emotion, though only a fool would think that to be true.

It's good, though. He's still in control. He needs all of his faculties about him to deal with the situation.

"There is danger everywhere around her, and everywhere around her people. Can't you see why I am doing this? Not only are they in danger, they have mutually beneficial resources that we could take advantage of. They have found a way to make use of the glass created from the impact of sky rocks on the sand. Not only that, they have discovered other useful things as well. And their leader in the city, Visidion—"

"I asked if you knew of her condition," Tashak interjects, cutting his attempt at making his case once more. "I have heard all of your reasoning, flawed as it is. I do not need to hear it again." He steps closer to Archion, two of the guards stepping up at his side, bracketing him. "I will ask only once more—did you know of her condition?"

His steady gaze locks with Archion's. I watch the battle of wills quietly, waiting, unsure of what I'll do no matter the outcome. It doesn't truly matter if Archion's will is stronger than the Councilor's.

The hierarchy is what it is. Perhaps outside, in the desert, it might matter. Here... whatever happens to Archion is at the Council's discretion. And Tashak's duty is to gather information. Which I know he will do at any cost.

Later, he will discuss what he found with the rest of the Council and they will report it up the lines. That is where the real executive power rests. This, this is only a debriefing.

Archion knows this, but I see him struggling to accept it.

Has he been gone so long from the Order? Has he forgotten how to stay in its hierarchy? It hasn't been that long that he's gone. It has to be the effect of his mate playing at his emotions—and his unborn child. That's the only thing that explains it.

Unfortunately, I doubt the Council will take in the extenuating circumstances if Archion deliberately rebels. The silence in the room is loud as we all watch Archion attempt to control himself. It takes a long moment, but he finally does so.

"I was unaware until this moment," he says clearly.

The words are a response to the question and only the question that was asked. Tashak stares at him a moment longer. Waiting to see if more is forthcoming? Wondering if Archion will actually lose control? I don't know.

After a moment, he breaks eye contact, stepping back with a sigh. Subtly, his face appears older, worn down, but only for a brief moment.

His mask slides firmly back into place and the Councilor, the person in charge, is there once again.

"Go inform the medic that he is to go see to the female and check on her well-being." He glances at Archion. "Also, he is to verify that she is actually carrying a human-Zmaj baby."

The wording of that is quite specific. The implications of which are insulting, at the very least. Does he think Nora would mate Archion and then have another's child?

"I have been trying to report that this was a possibility, but you would not listen," Archion returns in a frigid voice.

Tashak ignores it. Which is really the best outcome for

such a statement. Dropping my eyes I stare at the floor in front of my feet. The emotional storm of my thoughts rages on but I don't let it show outside. Riding through them is her. I can't stop seeing her face, the one they call Ashlee. Deep in my core, something stirs, and a fire ignites.

This... complicates everything.

12

ASHLEE

"*J*ust take deep breath. In. And out."

I rub Nora's back, watching the door Khal disappeared through. She wasn't feeling so hot even before he told her the news that we had to leave without Archion. The shock of it really wasn't good for her in her condition. I'm hoping at least the timing was good.

"What if they don't let us stay?" Nora mutters. "Not that I care, screw this place, but I'll be damned if I'm leaving without Archion!"

I'm worried about the same thing. I want to reassure her and tell her that there is no way they'll make us leave now, except I'm not so certain. It's not like we've been welcomed at all. It could be worse, by far, sure. I'm sure the Invaders wouldn't even be this friendly, but that's comparing apples and oranges.

"Don't borrow trouble," I say instead. It's a weak response and the deepening of her frown tells me she knows it. I try a slight smile. "Do you think they're afraid of pregnant women?"

She rolls her eyes, but a smile tugs at her lips.

"Maybe—"

The door bangs open and we both jump, startled. It isn't Khal this time.

"Archion!" Nora cries out, scrambling to her feet.

"Careful," I murmur, steadying her when she falters. "Don't move too fast."

Last thing we need right now is her to fall over and hurt herself. She's beyond hearing me at this point, already hurrying over to Archion. He closes the distance between them quickly, leaving behind the obvious escort of three robed and silent Zmaj guards who came with him. Three guards. A little overkill isn't it?

Unless they think Archion is really that dangerous. Or...they fully intend to keep him prisoner indefinitely. Okay, now I'm the one borrowing trouble.

Pointedly turning my back on the guards I watch Archion and Nora embracing each other tightly. Relief is obvious on both of their faces and in how desperately they're holding each other.

"They're telling us to leave without you," Nora says in a low voice.

Archion's muscles tense and he grimaces, his hands tightening on her. He deliberately relaxes his grip and his schools his face.

"Do not worry about that," he murmurs. An obvious sidestep. He pulls back and looks her over, holding her at arm's length. "Is it true?" he asks, frowning slightly. "Are you...do you carry our child?"

Nora tears up and her voice emerges a little choked.

"I didn't think about it until Ashlee said it, but...all the signs are there," she says, her lips trembling between a smile and a total breakdown.

"Oh, Nora," Archion murmurs, cupping her face with one hand.

His heart is in his eyes. The look he gives his mate is so tender that I look away, giving them some modicum of privacy. Closing my eyes I'm struck with an image of Khal drifting through my thoughts and a responding ache in my core.

"It's time," a deep voice growls.

The two of them should have privacy for this moment, but there is no privacy to be had here with the Order. Anger rises, hot and fast.

"Can't you twat-waddles give them a single minute? What's it going to hurt?" I bark, unable to keep it inside.

I know it won't help but damn it it's only a moment. The guard doesn't even spare me a glance, I might as well not have spoken. Closing my eyes I silently count to ten. Stupid, Ashlee, you're smarter than this.

"Move aside. I need to examine the female," a new voice says.

It carries an air of pomposity and self-entitlement with it that immediately turns me off. So much for giving them privacy. Opening my eyes there's a new Zmaj who is slightly slimmer than the rest, but that doesn't stop him from pushing Archion and the guards to the side.

He doesn't see Archion's face when he pushes him away from his pregnant mate, but I do. He's lucky he isn't dead on the spot.

"What are you doing?" Archion growls.

The Zmaj shakes his head, giving Nora a visual once-over.

"As I said, I have to give this female an examination. You can occupy yourself by cleaning that mess on the floor," he adds dismissively, jerking his chin toward the ground.

"Archion? Who the hell is this guy?" Nora asks, leaning away from the Zmaj.

Archion glares and if looks could kill and all that.

"He looks after the health of the Order. Medic I think you would say. And an herbalist."

"Yes, yes," the other man mumbles, reaching out for Nora's wrist. "Now...how do you feel? It is clear you felt ill earlier," he adds, looking at the floor.

"Yeah, I think my stomach is settling down," Nora responds tentatively. "Wait, what is that?"

He's holding a box that has a long tube emerging from it that ends in some kind of a wand. I've never seen anything like it.

"Simply a device to verify your condition," he reassures her.

I turn to Archion, who is watching like a hawk. Taking a step forward I lean in close, keeping my voice low, not that the guards won't notice, but whatever. It makes me feel better if nothing else.

"I'm guessing the meeting didn't go well?" I ask.

Archion doesn't look away from Nora.

"The conversation is...in progress," he says cryptically.

In progress? That's a new way to avoid answering.

"Are they going to make us leave without you?" I ask, trying to get something out of him. "Even though she's pregnant?"

He clenches his jaw and shakes his head.

"Protocol is very clear," he says clearly. "But I do not think they were anticipating such an occurrence."

"What does that mean?" I shake my head, moving on to another question. "Does this mean they didn't even want to talk about possible alliance?"

This time, he just makes a sound, a low grunt, his gaze fully on Nora. All right. I can read between the lines here. Things are going straight to shit. The political possibilities might be crumbling fast. The way they're treating us is a hint in and of itself.

If a sledgehammer could be called a hint. As soon as we stepped into the Order's territory, we completely lost control. And currently, shit is going down fast.

If we don't figure out some way to get these dragons to see matters differently, quickly, we won't even be able to get our foot in the door to have a discussion. I watch the medic and Nora.

He's scanning her with some handheld device with a metallic sheen, muttering something to himself. It really doesn't seem like Nora's condition is going to help us much here. We need another delay tactic, something that will appeal to whoever's in charge that will delay our departure.

Once we're gone, I don't know how we're to get back in, but nothing comes to me as we stand there awkwardly for a bit longer. Eventually the medic leaves, ostensibly with the information he came for. Then the guards take Archion away once more.

Nora and he embrace, this time briefly, and the guards are considerate enough to allow it. Or afraid enough, I'm not honestly sure which. They don't seem to want to tangle with Archion if they don't have to.

"Stay safe," Nora calls after him as he leaves, the worry in her eyes clear.

I put a comforting hand on her shoulder, but I don't know what to say that won't be a lie. So I stay silent. Fortunately, Khal arrives on the heels of their exit.

"I am certain that you two are ready to clean up after your long journey and..." He looks over at the mess on the floor that Archion did not clean up. Noticing that I snort, I don't blame him. The way the medic treated him, I wouldn't do what he said either. "I will have someone... clean that up," he continues, not finishing his last sentence. "In the meantime, would the two of you like to visit the bathing spring?"

Nora and I look at each other.

"Yes," Nora says immediately. "Water sounds like a good idea."

"Agreed," I chime in.

Khal nods, stepping over to one of the tapestries hanging close to a corner. Both of us watch as he pulls it back, revealing a small, hidden door. All right then, this place is more full of secrets than Hogwarts and I've literally seen only one room up to now. He looks over his shoulder to the two of us.

"Follow me," he says.

He doesn't wait for an answer, disappearing through the door that is just large enough for him to fit through with no space around him. I look into the dim interior of the tunnel he has revealed, just big enough for him to walk through slightly hunched over. Panic flutters, dark wings in my stomach, bile rising in my throat.

"You okay?" Nora asks.

"I'll go first," I volunteer, stepping through the doorway, quashing the rising fear.

Gritting my teeth, sweat beading my brow, I step into the tunnel. It's so... damn... close. Focus, Ashlee. One step, good, one more. Good. You got this, girl.

If anything is going to happen to us at the end of this tunnel, it's better I go first. I don't think this is anything but the bathing pool, but I'm finding it difficult to trust anyone here. Maybe because they're finding it so difficult to give us any benefit of the doubt.

Nora is my friend and she's pregnant. I'll be damned if I'm going to send the pregnant chick into the dark first. No matter how terrifying this small space is. Breathe deeper, right, it's hard, I know it. Keep breathing, in and out.

Nora steps in behind me and a dim shadow in front of me is all I see of Khal. His broad shoulders scrape the walls on either side. At least I'm not as big as he is. He barely fits inside. I'm distracted by the wet feel of the air and the sound of the water up ahead. Definitely water.

The tunnel leads down, though it isn't steep, and as we turn a corner it's well-lit as the tunnel we used to get up to the initial room. It isn't too long, maybe a minute later, the tunnel spits us out into a more spacious area with a high cavernous ceiling and multiple crystal-clear bubbling pools.

Obviously natural springs.

I immediately feel all the grime caked on me from our journey and then from staying in that room for as long as we have. I have been trying not to think too hard about how much of Nora's vomit splattered on my clothes. It was the least of my worries, but now that I'm confronted with water, all I want to do is rip off my clothes and jump into it.

"Nobody will disturb you here," Khal reassures us. "You may take your time. And there are drying cloths for you on the shelf near the tunnel."

He points. Suddenly I'm awkward and shy. Is he going to… watch? Is it wrong that a small part of me wants him to? Stopping the runaway train of my thoughts as I suddenly imagine what he looks like under that robe, I turn away quickly, trying to cover the flush of my cheeks.

"Thank you," I murmur.

He turns and walks away. Daring a glance in his direction, he goes back into the tunnel and disappears.

Unbuttoning my shirt I'm more than ready to head into the water. Quickly stripping, I dip my toes into the pool. It's warm but not too warm. There are carved steps leading into the water. Nora moved quicker than I have and she's already treading water.

"This is great!" she exclaims, ducking her head under.

I'm about halfway down when I feel a prickle of awareness. Turning back toward the tunnel my gaze clashes with Khal's. His eyes drop down to the good amount of cleavage revealed above the water, his gaze heating. My breath catches in my throat, but he turns away again and disappears through the tunnel without a word.

I let out the breath that caught in my throat. It felt good to be looked at like that, and I feel the same attraction that he apparently does. It's often a matter of reflex, something that we can't really control. Either attraction is there, or it isn't. I can't deny the charge between us since the beginning, before he stamped it out with duty.

He is clearly the uptight sort, the type to always follow the rules, the kind who takes protocol very, very seriously. But...

As far as I'm concerned, there are always loopholes. Always ways to skirt around the letter of the law. I'm all for towing the line when it suits the situation. Sometimes though, I have to get creative. We need one another, the dragons of this Order and our human-Zmaj hybrid territories.

We share a common enemy, have resources that we can trade between us, and the hope of a future for both of our races.

Fact is, the writing on the wall is very clear. There aren't enough humans to ensure the survival of our race. The Zmaj may have it even worse with no females. No way for their line to live on without us. Those are all cold hard facts. One that the Order doesn't seem ready to face.

Beyond even all of that, it might sound cheesy, but the truth is...love always prevails over worn-out traditions. Heck, we've seen it time and time again with all of the matings that have happened. With the mating that happened between Archion and Nora now.

If the Order can't see that the future is inevitable, they're deliberately closing their eyes to it. If there's anything I've learned so far, it's that being too rigid is a death sentence.

The mining settlement finally realized that, mostly. Hopefully the Order will also realize it, without so much drama.

For now, I shelve it in favor of kicking off into the water and swimming out to Nora. We splash and laugh, letting the tension of the past few hours slip away. We have some fun then swim to the side, letting the warm water loosen knotted muscles.

"God, that feels good," Nora sighs, resting her head back against the edge of the pool.

"Yeah," I agree, lowering myself up to my neck. "I feel like I haven't bathed in weeks."

She nods, her face suffusing with more color. I'm glad to see it. Stress can't be good for her in this condition, but there really is no help for it. We scrub ourselves off with the sand at the bottom of the spring before floating for a while. Then it's time to clean our clothes.

"I can wash my own," Nora protests when I grab hers as well.

I wave her away.

"I'll be done in a second," I reassure her. "You just rest."

She shakes her head.

"Thanks, Ashlee," she murmurs. When I turn to look at her, her eyes are on me. "I don't know how I would've gotten through any of this without you here too."

I shake my head.

"You would've gotten through it," I say, confident in my answer. "You're stronger than you're giving yourself credit for."

"Maybe, but it doesn't mean that I don't appreciate you."

"Well, maybe you can name the baby after me," I quip.

I grin when she laughs.

"A baby," she sighs, rubbing her still-flat stomach. "I still can't wrap my head around it."

I nod, understanding that. What would it be like?

Knowing you have something growing inside of you? Especially something that is a product of the love she and Archion have for each other?

"I don't even know where we're going to live," Nora adds, frowning.

"Don't think about that now," I urge. "Those are just details. You guys will figure it out."

She nods, but I can see the stress seeping back to her face. There's no help for it. There's no way not to be stressed in a situation like this, when she's separated from her mate and she doesn't know what's going to happen. Done washing the clothes, I lay them out flat to dry. They'll probably take longer here than they would in the room where it's not as humid.

I slide back into the water where we stay for quite a bit, enjoying the feel of it lapping against my skin. Eventually, even we have to throw in the proverbial towel. We're beyond pruney.

Pulling ourselves out, we make our way over to the tunnel entrance. Grabbing one of the largest drying cloths from the shelf Khal pointed out, I dry myself off and then wrap it around me for the trek back to the room.

Nora does the same. Then we grab our clothes and trudge back up the tunnel. We find some hooks on the other side that we hang our clothes on.

"I hope they dry fast," Nora murmurs, re-tucking the drying cloth. "I don't feel very secure wrapped in a towel."

"I hear you," I agree, lowering myself onto a cushion. "At least they're comfortable."

She nods, joining me on one of the cushions.

"True."

Luckily, I guess, we're left alone for a quite a while. Hours slip by without event. It's long enough that the clothes are dry enough that we put them back on. Eventually, we both combine cushions and lie down to wait.

"I can't sleep," Nora murmurs into the silence.

"Just rest then," I urge her. "We need to all we can."

She sighs, shifting on the cushions.

"Okay."

Neither of us sleeps, but we lie there for maybe another hour before the door opens. Both of us sit up, Nora looking hopeful, but her expression falls when Khal walks through the door.

At least he has food with him. He carries a tray laden with steaming containers to the low table, setting them out carefully.

My stomach rumbles in response as I look at the array of meat dishes, vegetables, and what looks like some kind of rice maybe. I'll say one thing, they aren't trying to starve us.

"Where is Archion?" Nora demands.

Khal straightens, his face impassive.

"He will return to you soon enough," he reassures her.

"What does that mean?" I ask. "Tonight? Tomorrow? Two days from now?"

"All I can say is soon enough," he returns.

Nora and I look at each other. I would get mad, but I don't think he's the one in charge here.

"Okay," I agree, speaking for both of us. "We're willing to wait for as long as it takes. I am certain the Council will...see the value of peace in this situation."

An odd expression crosses his face. His eyes lock on mine then slide down toward my chest. Does he shiver? It's a moment only but then his mask slides firmly back in place in an instant. That probably doesn't bode well for a good outcome here.

"Enjoy your meal," he murmurs, backing away toward the door. "I must leave."

Then he's gone once more and we're alone.

"Well. He was eager to leave our company," Nora observes.

"Yeah," I agree, looking at the closed door thoughtfully. I turn back to her. "You should eat something."

She shakes her head, standing up.

"I don't even want to look at the food right now," she informs me, pacing the length of the small room. "If I take even one bite it isn't going to end well."

"I understand, but try to eat something. Maybe one of these things—they look kind of bland."

It actually looks like a cracker of some kind. She takes it from me.

"Thank you," she says, taking a small nibble of the crunchy thing.

She chews for a moment then swallows. She takes another bite. Good.

"Maybe you can sit and have a couple of bites of something else," I start.

She shakes her head.

"I need to keep walking. It feels as if my whole world has been turned upside down in an instant. I don't want to sit."

"Fair enough."

She looks over at me apologetically.

"Sorry," she mutters. "I'm not in the best mood."

"You're allowed."

I don't know who would be more allowed. She shakes her head.

"It looks like we might have come all this way for nothing."

"Maybe. Maybe not."

She looks over at me.

"What do you mean?"

I shrug.

"I mean, you are carrying one of their bloodline. An alliance feels almost inevitable in that case, even if only a weak, surface one at first. I can't see how a shift of perspective is eminent in this case. Maybe it won't happen right away, but I think it will happen."

"I hope you're right," she says, the worry not leaving her face.

I hope so too. Grabbing one of the bowls, I serve myself some of the food. Taking a bite, I can't help but make a noise of appreciation.

"Good?" Nora asks, watching me.

I nod enthusiastically. It's deeply flavored, so good that I can't help but wonder at the quality of the food they have here in general.

"There is meat, but there's also vegetables in here that I've never seen," I say, swallowing the bite in my mouth. "Another reason to build an alliance with these people."

Nora sits down and I ladle some of the stew into a bowl for her.

"It does smell good," she agrees, taking the bowl. I didn't fill it as far up as I filled my own. "Thank you. I hope I can keep it down."

"Just go slowly. Maybe have some of those crackers while you do."

I wonder if they sent those specifically because of her state. I watch her eat it, relieved when she keeps it down. The food really is good. I'm guessing the origin of it is another secret I won't find out on this particular journey.

But if we can figure out how to get the Council to agree to a meeting... matters may very well be different sooner rather than later.

That's a big if. Fingers crossed.

13

KHAL

I carefully maintain my distance from the females. I oversee their meal preparation, bathe separately in the spring, do everything I can to keep that so-necessary space between us. Between the emerald-eyed woman and myself, if I am honest.

Even now, when I am not around her, she has a way of slipping into my head, overtaking my thoughts without trying. In truth, I do not know how to deal with this. Focus comes easily to me in the usual course of events. Even when I feared Archion was lost, I was able to do what needed to be done.

But this, this is new territory for me.

She is beautiful. Her head covered with thick, silky hair, soft skin that lacks any scales whatsoever and that utterly feminine body. I shouldn't have looked back, but I couldn't resist the urge. Something has awakened, testing the limits of my control.

The moment I saw them... no, saw *her*, I'd wondered at the swell of her chest. Zmaj females did not have such a swollen chest. At first, I wondered if they had been injured, but they didn't move as if they had been. Curiosity was too much. I had to know.

No, that's not honest. Honesty with self is the first steps to enlightenment. I was curious about her. The other one—she is Archion's—there was nothing there that drew my curiosity. It was wrong. My scales itch as I recall the image of her walking into the water. My prime cock stiffens, rock hard and throbbing even as embarrassment colors my scales.

If it was just how she appeared, perhaps I would find it easier to ignore her, but it is more than that. The more time I am forced to spend with her, the more things I notice that I like. While Nora is understandably emotional and angry, Ashlee is calm and nonthreatening in the face of everything that has happened. Well composed. A trait I truly admire.

She is under a great deal of stress, but she does not let it show.

My instincts tell me that she is cognizant of the political maneuvering she must do to get what they came here for. That she is deliberately playing a role that she thinks will accomplish what she wants. Those same instincts tell me that she is also sincere even while playing this political game.

I don't blame her for planning her words and actions carefully. It is a natural and understandable reaction to the danger she finds herself in. Why would she be open and honest with her emotions and thoughts when she has stepped into a dangerous situation here?

I would be lying to myself if I didn't admit that I sympathize with her on a personal level. That softness that I can feel is one of the reasons I have not allowed myself more contact with her. She presents a clear danger to me. I cannot indulge myself in the lure of her delicate scent, cannot lose myself in that penetrating bright-green gaze. Cannot grow accustomed to the mesmerizing peace her presence seems to weave around me.

My cock throbs, jumping under my robes in time with the beating of my hearts. She is a challenge like nothing I have ever encountered before. I want to be near her too much. I do not trust myself. So I shield myself. I maintain my distance, only seeing her to bring meals, to take care of them as guests. Though, in this case, the line between guest and prisoner is thin indeed.

Pacing my quarters I try to find my center, that point of inner calm from which I remain in control. No matter how I try though, I see the image of her. The delicate swoop of her neck, that pale, soft skin leading down to her shoulder. The shocking mounds on her chest, full globes that look so soft. They bounced slightly as she turned to look at me and each of them was topped with small, perfect dark circles with hard-looking points standing out from them.

It's too much. I can't push it away. Ripping my robes aside I grab my prime cock firmly in my hand and stroke, examining every aspect of the image of her in my mind. Her eyes, sharp, piercing but an unmistakable fire burning in them. Desire, matching my own, calling to me.

My cock spasms and then my balls tighten, and my seed explodes from me with a force it never has before, spraying out as my balls squeeze and my cock pulses until at last it softens in my grip. My secondary cock stirs but that was enough to bring me back to my control place and I press down its desire for relief.

I'm in trouble and I have no idea how to handle this. How to handle her.

Right now, duty calls. Glancing at the counter on my side table, I am late for an appointment. Tashak will be interrogating Archion again, and I'm supposed to be close to hand. Quickly cleaning the mess I made, an empty ache in my core forms. But I push all that aside, then rush to my post.

"Again," Tashak's voice says through the door as I arrive.

The two guards on duty nod at my approach. Positioning myself between them I school my thoughts to patience and wait. Archion is giving the same story yet again. No flaws, which can only mean he's telling the truth. Eventually I know Tashak will see this. I only hope it will be enough to satisfy the Council.

There is no counter here but my internal time sense indicates at least an hour passes while I wait. The two guards and I are still as stones, no outward motion to give away that we're more than statues. Another piece of our training. Any of us could stand so for hours on end, not blinking an eye. Watching, our awareness stretching out to take in every signal the environment offers us.

Something changes in the air. Someone inside the room is moving closer to the door. There's a shift in the currents of the air that gives it away. As expected, the door opens, although it's Tashak himself.

"Take him to his mate," he orders, looking at me.

"Of course," I respond, saluting with fist into palm and giving a slight bow.

Tashak frowns, eyes cold before he turns and walks away. Archion is standing behind him, shackles on his hands. One of the guards inside the room walks over and removes them. Archion ignores everyone in the room and walks to me, rubbing his wrists. A simple nod is all the greeting we give each other, but he is my brother and that nod conveys much more than anyone else could read.

"I think perhaps Tashak is softening on the matter," he murmurs in a low voice, a spark of hope in his eyes.

"Perhaps," I agree, not wanting to grow his hope too much for fear that it is unwarranted.

He stops in front of me, close enough that I can see every speck of color in his eyes. I can see everything in his gaze. The fact that he meant no offense to the directive. The fact that he has kept the Order's secrets despite what I am certain was immense pressure from his mate's people. And that he could not have done things differently if he tried.

He found his mate and made his claim. A natural and inevitable conclusion in such a scenario.

I see all of this with no further words exchanged. I know my brother. Know that nothing beyond extreme and unique circumstances would ever lead him astray from the protocols, the laws put in place to maintain the Order's secrecy. I only wish I could do more to help him. The fact is, I have no power. I am not in a regulatory position, cannot make any decisions on the matter.

I doubt Tashak will even ask my opinion, assuming my judgment is not to be trusted as my brother is the subject of the issue. And... perhaps that is for the best.

Even if he did ask me, I am not at all certain what my answer would be. I fully sympathize with Archion, with the predicament he has found himself in. However, I also understand the reasoning behind the stringent code of conduct. The decision made here could affect more than just this contingent of the Order. We cannot threaten the peace between the territories of the Order.

A softer reaction may result in rifts or cracks in the foundation that keeps the secrets of Tajss out of the wrong hands. There is much more to consider here than Archion or his pregnant mate.

The Council Seers will need to make the decision with utmost care and consideration—there is no other way to move forward. The only thing I can currently take real solace in is that they do not seem intent on punishing Archion beyond the humiliations he has already endured thus far. If they wanted to make an example of him, warn the others off of such a route, they could have. At least there is that.

However, it is still not a good sign that the questioning is continuing for so long. I fear that the Council may very well send Archion back with Nora and Ashlee, banishing him from the Order's territory. A harsh punishment for anyone, especially someone like Archion, who I know cares more about the Order than anyone I can think of, but intent is not always the most important factor, is it?

In real life, matters are almost always gray. I carefully sequester my thoughts in a corner of my mind, where I hope they will stay, will not continue to tug at the reserve of emotion that I would rather not succumb to. Emotion is a luxury, one that Archion is currently paying the price for.

My duty is to the Order. It is as clear now as it has always been. This is the true test, is it not? I cannot fail in the face of true conflict or my loyalty was never very strong. The Council's decision will be final and I will adhere to the protocol they set forth on this matter when they are ready to issue it.

There is no other option, except as we walk it hits me that I'm about to see her again. My chest tightens at the thought and I'm suddenly anxious.

When we arrive at their room, I step to one side. Archion looks askance but I shake my head and motion that he should go in. I can't see her, not at this moment. I'm not sure I could keep my center if I do. An insane urge is rising inside of me to grab the females and run, run far from the Order, take them away anywhere. Perhaps back to their city or deep into the desert. So deep the Order could never find us.

Stupid. It's a terrible idea if for no other reason I know the Order would never stop looking. Beyond that there is no call for such action. They are not in danger, nor is Archion, nor I. Archion walks through the door while I move to one side. I don't want to catch even a glimpse of her. The temptation she presents is too much.

The four guards take up positions up and down the hallway. Ready and alert. So many guards is really overly dramatic, but I do not have any input on the matter. Does Tashak truly believe that Archion is going to attack someone?

"Tashak wants you," one of the guards says out of nowhere.

"What?" I ask. He turns his head to me without moving his body. His frown says it all without repeating the words. "Right."

The door to the holding room is closed. Soft voices that I can't make out, but I recognize Nora and Archion. Straining my senses I listen for her voice to no avail. Fire flames in my core and I know, with total certainty, I could take the four guards easily. The door is no barrier. I would be through it before they could react. Archion would act with me and we would be gone.

Stupid. Idiotic. My duty is to the Order. Period.

Turning sharply I hasten back to the Councilors' chambers. When I reach it the door is closed so I knock.

"Khal—please come inside."

Walking in, Tashak is seated at his desk. He looks up when I step inside.

"Yes?" I ask, saluting and bowing a half-bow.

"I need you to ensure your brother and the females remain sequestered here at the edge of the Outpost. They are a distraction. Better they be kept out of sight of the Order's operations until we reach a decision on this matter."

I nod.

"I understand," I respond, not at all surprised at the request. "Is there anything else?"

"No. You may take care of this matter now."

I salute again and give another nod before stepping out of the open doors of the chamber.

Walking slowly back to where Archion and the females are staying I focus my thoughts, finding my center. No more of the crazy primal drives. They are not me. Animalistic, base, and I am above them. My duty is clear, and I will not act against it. No matter how soft and delicate…

No. I am in control.

Passing the four guards still at their posts I go to the door and don't bother knocking before entering. Ashlee rises as soon as I enter the room. Someone already brought their next meal to them, because the table full of food.

Nora is resting her head on Archion's chest. He has his arms wrapped around her, holding her protectively close. My gaze goes to Ashlee, only to find her eyes already upon mine. I look away, taking a step back toward the door. The fire in my gut rages into an inferno, trying to melt away my reason and duty.

"Stay," Archion says as I move toward the door. "Join us in our meal."

I shake my head. It is not a good idea for me in the state I find myself in.

"I cannot," I say. "I have duties to see to."

Out of the corner of my eye I see Ashlee slowly lower herself back onto the floor cushion, making an understanding sound. I can almost feel disappointment radiating off of her. Why is it so difficult for me to keep my thoughts in order when she is in the vicinity?

She is but a female. I am stronger than this.

"The offer is always open." Her voice rings in the room as I turn toward the door. I pause. "Nora is the family of my heart and you are her mate's brother. You don't choose love. It just is."

When I turn around, she is not looking at me, reaching forward to scoop the prepared stew into her bowl. Lower warrior regiments take turns cooking in kitchen shifts. The food is simple but good, but the food does not matter here.

I want to stay, want to soak in her presence too much for

me to trust myself. I suppress the turmoil of emotions raging as I wrestle with myself.

"My thanks," I return, addressing her. I see Nora and Archion noting the exchange, but this is between me and Ashlee.

My voice comes out less gruffly, softer than I intend it to. She looks up at me, meeting my eyes. She is brave in a different way than I am accustomed to. Unafraid to love openly and without suspicion.

It is not something I have encountered before, nothing quite this way. It stirs something within me that I am unsure I am prepared or ready for, but that I also cannot keep my mind off of for long. I nod at her and she nods back just as gravely.

There is no need for me to be quite so rough in my discourse with Ashlee. It is not listed in the protocols and I find I want to be softer with her. I turn away and finally leave quietly through the door.

I will maintain my distance, but perhaps I will not fight my instinct to be soft with her quite so hard.

14

ASHLEE

*M*y gaze lingers on the closed door. On some level I could almost sense an internal conflict in Khal about whether or not to stay, even for something as simple as a meal. Maybe I'm reading more into it than is there. Worse, maybe I'm projecting my own feelings onto him, but I don't think so.

I wanted him to stay. Something in him calls to something in me. Which is great—exactly the kind of distraction I need right now. Why don't I go all gaga in the middle of the most delicate negotiation I've ever been a part of and my one opportunity to prove myself to Rosalind and Visidion. Beautiful, let my hormones do my thinking.

Except it's more than that. Frowning, I chew on the inside of my cheek, turning my thoughts and feelings over in my mind. Dragging them out of the dark corners of my mind I've been shoving them into. I've got time. The two lovers are completely enraptured in each other next to me. One quick glance reassures me of that. Archion is feeding Nora bits of food as she sprawls across his body where they lie on the pillows.

My cheeks flush. I wish I could give them some privacy but I'm not sure it's going to matter to them much longer. If her hand goes any lower and I'm pretty sure I'll get to be a witness to their reunion festivities.

If Khal were here too then we could...

Oh jeez, stop it, Ashlee. Don't be a twat-waffle.

Averting my gaze from them I refill my plate and subtly sit back down to maximize the small amount of privacy I can give them. Which, of course, isn't much since we're in a ten-by-ten room. Eating slowly, I occupy myself with dissecting my own thoughts and feelings.

Khal is obviously committed to his duty to the Order. I respect that, but I also feel a disappointment that's too great for the situation. I don't know him, but I can't deny the shift in my mood when he refused to stay.

When we first met out there in the desert, his eyes locked on me and something electric happened. It passed between the two of us. What was that? At first, I wrote it off to a natural reaction to seeing a sexy man. My body reacting, nothing new, sometimes a great-looking guy hits me that way. Having a momentary desire to bang a guy isn't this though, and looking at that moment in hindsight, it was something more. Much more.

What? What more?

A connection? Love at first sight?

I snort then choke on the mouthful of food. Tears form in my eyes as I cough more, trying to clear the obstruction. A glass of water is shoved at me and a hand pounds on my back. Gasping after I clear my airway, I wipe the tears and look up to Archion's massive form dwarfing me.

"Thanks." I force the words out, my throat and chest raw from that stupid mistake.

He smiles, nods, then returns to sit next to Nora. I'm

thankful he's back, for her sake if nothing else. She was suffering too much without him.

Having been ripped apart and then finding out she was pregnant only to be ripped apart again, and now with so much uncertainty... Yeah. Stressful to say the least.

"You okay?" Nora asks, worry on her face.

"Yeah," I say, a coughing spasm gripping me once more.

I drink more water and the pain eases, angry muscles finally relaxing. They both watch to make sure I really am. A warmth floods through me. These are my friends. They care about me and I care about them. How did we get to this point?

The same way anybody does. We talked, we shared, and we have common ground together. I don't have any of that with Khal, so why the hell do I feel like I do?

I'm going in a circle that I need to break out of, so I do the only thing I can. I bring up the elephant in the room. Sorry guys, I'd really rather not watch you two get it on anyway.

"Any progress with Tashak?" I ask.

Archion's jaw clenches at the question and his eyes narrow.

"Tashak is finding it difficult to listen to reason," he responds, refilling his plate.

A cryptic answer, but I'm surprised he answered so easily. If I had to guess, I'd say it's due to the fact that he's furious under the calm façade he presents. It's really impressive for a Zmaj to be able to harness such a strong emotion so well. Such a strong fire, such a strong reaction, can easily lead to the bijass—the animalistic aspect of Zmaj nature—gaining control. Perhaps these guys of the Order aren't just strong physically.

"Do you think he'll come around eventually?" I try, ready to use it to my advantage if he wants to talk.

"I do not know what he will decide. All I know is that I am tired of answering the same questions again and again."

Nora covers his hand with her own.

"I'm sorry they're reacting so badly to me," she murmurs.

His expression softens as he covers her hand with his own.

"You have nothing to apologize for," he counters, his heart in his eyes as he looks at his mate. "Absolutely nothing. If anyone should be humbling themselves, it is Tashak."

Rage crosses his eyes before he quickly brings it under control. An ache forms in my throat watching them and I want to say something, but I don't have any words of comfort to offer.

Frankly, I'm surprised he's holding it together at all. Protocols or not, I can't understand why it would be necessary to separate the two of them. They're mates. They're supposed to be joined at the hip, especially now that they're expecting. Are they so far removed from their emotional selves here that they can't see that? Or do they just refuse to do so?

"Is Tashak going to allow you to stay? Let us stay?" I ask, not wanting to break up the tender moment, but having to be practical.

Who knows when they'll send Khal back in to take Archion away? We need to take advantage of this time now. Archion frowns, turning back to me.

"Tashak is not the one who will ultimately decide our fate," he informs me. "The Council will decide what will be done with us." He turns back to Nora, raising his hand to her face, meeting her eyes with his own. "But no matter what they decide, I know I will be wherever my mate and my child are."

Nora smiles, the worry in her eyes clear.

"I know," she whispers. "I know."

Good. My heart lifts at his clear intention and desire to remain with his mate and child. It's not a surprise, but seeing the others here...

The Order—their indoctrination—is a completely different kind of beast. The thought raises another point that I've been worrying over.

"If they decide to... Can they separate the two of you?" I ask, knowing it's something that's been on Nora's mind as well.

How could it not be? Archion shakes his head.

"No. There are no protocols that can be used against a familial tie. I am certain of this. I have read them all more than once."

I'm sure he has. Biting my lip, I think over his words. It's small tidbits of information out of which I'm trying to create a whole. The protocols. A Council that will decide what to do with us. Pieces of a whole.

"Is there going to be a vote about what happens?" I ask. "Is that how it works?"

He nods.

"Yes. Only one vote is needed to require a meeting. It will go to the Council and then possibly be taken before all our brethren, or it could go... higher."

Higher? All the brethren? Something about the way he says that... There's an implication there that leaves me reeling. Leaning back into the pile of pillows, I take a moment to try and wrap my mind around an ambiguity that isn't coming clear.

I'm sure there's more meaning in those words than I'm fully grasping. They're simple words, but his tone of voice, his posture, the look in his eyes... I'm missing something. At the very least it sounds like something that would be best avoided.

Hmm.

I try to contain my excitement as the ramifications run through my mind. A loophole. We have a loophole. And his name is Khal.

We have to find a way to secure this stoic dragon as our contingency plan. If the higher-ups vote and the whole thing goes sideways, he can potentially break that tie. If all the "brethren" get a vote, how many would we need to vote in our favor? Khal is our one resource that could reach outside these four walls.

Of course, it's easier said than done. He seems to be trying his best to stay away from us, from me. Which I hate to admit bothers me, but it does. Still, this is the only way I can see, our one shot of hope. It's either that or escape, which isn't really an option. The Order is obviously powerful, and failing to find a diplomatic solution could bring war to Tajss, again.

I have to find a way to motivate him to vote for what is right, vote in our favor. I'm hoping it won't be too much of an uphill battle to stand up for his brother's right to officially welcome Nora, without a whole bunch of trouble from his own people.

Not only would it help Nora and Archion, it could potentially free us up to explore this heady magnetism between the two of us. Right now, I think he's fighting it too. An internal struggle between how we are drawn to each other and what he is duty-bound to do.

I have to find a way to change that, tip the balance so to speak. Assuming I'm right. But if I'm not, then we're screwed. Nope, this must work.

Playing out every possible scenario I can dream up the hours pass by slowly. Archion and Nora are absorbed in each other, which is fine if a bit boring for me. Lying down with my back to them is the most I can give them, so I do that and consider every action and reaction that might possibly happen.

I don't know how much time passes, but my stomach is starting to grumble softly when the door scrapes open. Khal fills the opening, a dark figure with the light behind him.

"What is it?" Archion asks, rising to his feet, staring at his brother.

"The Council has agreed we are not monsters. You and Nora will be allowed to bathe in private. I am to escort Ashlee to the pools so she may bathe as well," he says in a neutral voice.

Did I detect the slightest of vibratos to his words? As if it's about to crack? My pussy is instantly wet and my heart beats faster. Alone. At the pools. With him.

This is my chance.

"Brother?" Archion asks.

It's a simple word, nothing to construe about it, but only an idiot would miss the fact that in one single word he and Khal are having a much deeper conversation.

"It's fine," Khal says.

His eyes never leave Archion. Not once does he even glance in my direction. A good sign or a bad one?

The two of them continue their staring match, and I sense they're communicating through body language or for all I know flat-out telepathy. The world is getting weirder after all. Archion nods his agreement finally and holds a hand out to Nora, helping her to her feet.

I climb to my own feet, no one bothering to offer me a hand. Khal steps out of the door to let his brother and Nora pass, then it is just us. The guards outside the door trail after Archion, leaving us truly alone.

"Hi," I say, lifting a hand then dropping it to my side.

I can't meet his eyes. They're too... perfect. Deep, swirling pools that make my heart skip and my lungs forget to breathe. When I let my eyes dart to his face and away, he seems to be having the same problem.

Or so I hope.

It could be he finds me repulsive. Maybe not all Zmaj are into human women? Is Khal the exception to the rule?

Fuck me, if he is, we're beyond screwed. My plan would be shot to hell and back.

"Please, follow me," he murmurs, not looking at me directly as he ushers me toward the door that leads to the spring.

"Sure, thanks," I say, following his broad back. Well, it's now or never. "So, is this where you bathe too?" I ask as we enter the humid cavern holding the spring.

"No," he says shortly, turning to move toward the tunnel.

"Do you guys have a lot of springs underground here?" I ask, starting to unbutton my shirt.

He stops and I see him take a deep breath as his shoulders rise and then slowly fall. He turns around and looks at me. A storm rages in his purple eyes.

"We have a decent amount," he replies, his eyes dropping to the triangle of chest I've exposed. I don't stop unbuttoning, watching his face.

"Do you believe love should be separated by rules and protocols, Khal?" I ask softly, trailing my fingers down the swath of exposed skin. His eyes are hot as he stares at that skin, my shirt just covering the tips of my breasts but exposing the rounded curves of my cleavage. It takes him some time to raise his eyes back up to my face, and when he does the edges of his scales are brighter, his eyes glittering.

He stares long and hard and the air is crackling between us. My own breath catches, my heart beating faster. Will he give in? Will he admit that his leaders here are wrong, claim me the way we both clearly want him to?

He swallows, shakes his head, and starts to turn away.

Every muscle in my body tenses and my nostrils flare. I grab his hand, as if I could physically stop him from leaving if I wanted to. I don't know what I'm expecting.

He whirls around. Cold fear runs over me as he grabs my arms and lifts me off my feet. I'm less than an inch from his eyes. My breath bursts from my lungs at the abrupt movement, my eyes widen, but that's all the time I have to react.

The next instant, his hand is tangled in my hair and his mouth is on mine. All thoughts leave my head as he kisses me with a passion I've never experienced before. His taste fills me, the feel of his body against me, the hard and sure way he crushes against my body.

My whole body is on fire, tingles running throughout. Is this what he was feeling all along? How has he been holding back? With a sigh, I soften against him. My mouth molds against his as I slide my hands up his muscled arms, but he pulls away, completely out of my arms, setting me back on the ground.

My now-empty hands tingle and I drop them, then open my eyes. His burn with a fire that matches my own. His mouth parts as he draws in quick breaths, but then he takes a deep breath and lets it out slowly, his mask settling onto his face.

"This is inappropriate," he says harshly.

I don't know if he is trying to convince me or himself. I'm not sure even he knows.

I take a step toward him, hot, wet air brushing against my bare skin.

"Is it?" I ask, my whisper loud in the quiet.

He stares, clearly struggling with himself, and there's no denying the massive tent in his loose robes just below his waist. I watch the war in his eyes, between desire and duty. His body quivers, his hands start to rise, but ultimately he falls on the side of duty.

Silent, he turns and leaves, leaving me to bathe in the spring alone. Gritting my teeth I turn my back to the tunnel. His loss.

Except it's not his alone. It's mine. The coiled spring in my core pounds desire with every beat of my heart. Blood burns hot and I still taste his lips on mine, feel the pressure of his hard, muscled body pressed into mine.

Screw it.

Sliding out of my clothes, not caring if he's watching or anyone else is, I sit down on the edge of the warm water. Sliding partway in, enough that the water comes to my waist, I run my hands over my stomach and down between my legs.

Pressing hard against my opening I apply pressure to my clit, closing my eyes and holding onto the memory of what happened.

As soon as I touch myself a gasp escapes. My heart doubles its beating and in only two or three rubs I'm breathing in shallow, soft moans. His hands. So strong, gripping me tight. His mouth claiming mine.

Claiming me.

Never in my life has one kiss, one moment been so passionate, so filled with desire, or so dominating.

Pressing harder, I slide one finger inside myself and my body explodes. Muscles tighten, toes curl, my back arches, and I slide into the water up to my neck. The warmth of the springs adds a layer of sensation as my nipples are covered by it.

I'm left shaking and gasping in air as the orgasm passes.

Floating, alone, I know. I have to make him see. I have to make Khal mine.

15

KHAL

I wait in the tunnel, far enough inside that I cannot see into the cavern holding the spring, but I do hear the splashing of the water, the sounds of Ashlee bathing. I try not to think about her naked and wet just behind me, but it is a losing battle.

I take a deep breath, trying to slow the racing of my heart, the thoughts that keep wanting to invade. No. I must remain strong. Must remain disciplined. I keep repeating this to myself, though it is not as successful as I would hope. Meaning, not successful at all.

Clenching my fists tight enough that my nails draw blood, I struggle to remain in control. Duty wars with desire. My prime cock throbs, demanding its need be met, but I am of the Order. I am trained and will not fold.

"Ahhh." Her voice echoes off the stone walls of the tunnel.

I rush forward, certain something is wrong. The sound wasn't one of pain, or fear, but why would she cry out?

I'm not out of the tunnel when I see her leaning against the edge of the pool. Her hand is between her legs while the other is running over the swell of her oddly exposed and incredibly erotic breasts. She moans again and now it's clear that the sound is one of pleasure.

Staring, my hearts stop, no breath. I don't move a muscle.

Is she?

Her body arches and thrashes in the water. She is.

As her body breaks the water soft fur comes into view between her legs where her hand works furiously. In this aspect she is akin to what I recall of Zmaj females. Her breasts, soft mounds that are open and exposed, are an erotic delight and nothing like the Zmaj females were when they existed. My mouth waters and my fingers tingle at the thought of touching them, tasting them.

She rubs furiously between her legs and there is no more resistance possible. Pulling up my robe I grab my prime and stroke, moving in time with her own stroking. She's moving fast and I won't last long.

Her moans grow louder. I bite my tongue to keep silent, not wanting to give away that I'm watching her in this private moment, that I'm participating to some degree. My balls pull tight as I stroke faster, harder. She's building to an edge and I'm right there with her.

She moans then cries out, a long low sound that echoes off the stone walls. Her body arches, her stroking stops, and in that moment of her release I let my own go as well. My seed flies out, splattering on the stone wall and dripping to the ground. It continues to pump out, more than I've ever seen, going on and on.

Finally it finishes at the same time as she lowers back into the water and floats. I step back farther into the tunnel, unwilling to be seen. I retreat up the tunnel and wait. Eventually I hear Ashlee exit the water and her footsteps drawing closer toward the drying cloths.

Everything in me wants to turn around, wants to walk over to her. Wants to finish what she started only moments ago, but I do not. I hold strong, cling to my duty. Cling to my sense of self. It is painful.

When I hear the rustle of clothes being put on, I carefully compose my face. She must not know how much her advance affected me or that I saw her in her moment of privacy. I must remain strong against any further attempts on her part. I can't give in to her. If I did I know I'd betray the Order and I can't do that.

Stilling myself, I turn around when I hear her much lighter footsteps enter the tunnel. She glances at me only briefly before continuing on past me.

"You didn't have to wait for me," she informs me, cool tones over her usually warm voice.

Surprised at the turn, I do not follow her immediately, but when she continues walking, I quickly take a few steps to close the distance between us.

"You require an escort while here in Order territory," I return.

She nods stiffly, not even turning her head to look at me. I frown at her delicate profile, at a loss. This is not the Ashlee that I have grown to know over the last two days. She seems upset. Upset on a deeper level than I can fathom.

For the first time, her company is cold. The walk back from the spring leaves me...uneasy. And not because of the tingles of attraction I've come to expect between us. I remain silent next to her as we continue to walk, pondering this change and how much I do not like it.

The Order has trained me to assume I do not need love. The Order is enough to meet all of my needs. It is a truth, a fact that I have never questioned. The Devastation reinforced the idea for me. The Order is the only reason that I am still alive, that I still have purpose after the fall of our civilization.

And yet.

And yet.

I look over at Ashlee once more. I would be deluding myself if I continued to deny that this woman does not light up every circuit within me. That her cunning and wit do not draw my admiration, do not filter into my dreams, into my consciousness. I have been unable to curtail thoughts of her for days now. Long enough to know that I will not be able to.

And now, after that kiss...

The thought of it, of my duty to the Order, is not quite so strong, fading into the background as thoughts of claiming Ashlee for my own take its place. I cannot stop thinking about the passion with which I would take her. How I would touch her. How I would worship her.

I feel like a changed man when we open the door and enter the room with Archion and Nora. She walks me to the door leading out. I turn to the object of my obsession, not knowing what I want to say, but needing to say something.

"Thank you," she says curtly.

I feel the loss of her warmth like a blow.

"Ashlee—"

"Good night," she murmurs, soft and final.

Before I can respond with any words of my own, she closes the door. I stare at the hard barrier. I'm more alone than I can ever remember feeling. Sighing, I turn away. I suppose I deserve it.

There is no point in running from myself anymore. The emotional armor that I believed I was erecting against Ashlee was a deception from the beginning. A lie I let myself believe. The truth is, the moment I laid eyes on her, I have not been able to rest.

No amount of sparring, of considering the possible promotion, or anything else that was once a goal or dream penetrates the cloud of emotion that rose in me upon her entrance into my life. My chest aches hard enough I wonder if I took a hit I missed in training. I am beginning to think that I might understand exactly what Archion experienced with Nora.

And... perhaps it is worth fighting for, but I cannot do anything about that now.

Replaying every moment we've been together in my thoughts, I storm away to my room. Slamming the door behind me I pace the small space that is allotted as mine. This can't be happening, not now, not ever. Rolling my shoulders to relieve the tension doesn't work.

Perhaps I can fight off my frustrations by expending energy against the other Zmaj warriors there to practice. Leaving my rooms, I make my way to the sparring rings. There's a lower warrior lingering, waiting for a partner, so I nod to him. He nods back and we step into an area of hard packed sand marked out for bouts.

We pace off, stop and stare at each other, then salute. The moment he straightens I attack, rushing in close, throwing fast jabs with my fists. He backs up on the defense. Feinting with my left I swing my tail right and sweep his feet out from under him. He goes down hard, his head slamming against the ground. He doesn't move fast enough and before he can rise again I pin him until he concedes defeat.

Rising off of him I offer a hand. He takes it and I pull him to his feet.

"Train more," I say. "Harder."

"Yes sir," he says, saluting me again and leaving the ring.

As I'm turning to look for another partner someone calls my name.

"Khal!"

I turn and see Typhon, Thargar, and Reoz watching me from the far side of the arena. They are higher warriors, a group that does not usually deal much with midrange warriors like myself, but they have been attempting to be more inclusive, inviting me into their fold more as of late.

A result of Tashak's approval, perhaps. Their attention is enough to cut through the doubts. I nod then walk over to them. I can't deny it is an honor for a midrange warrior to be considered for a higher seat. Their attention is a sign of my progression in the ranks of the Order.

"Good fight," Typhon comments. "Perhaps you need someone with some more experience, though. He didn't really present a challenge, now did he?"

"Perhaps," I agree. I gesture toward another open practice space. "Would you like to spar?"

An easy grin spreads across his face, arrogance beaming. It's a common trait among most of the higher warriors. They've earned it, of that there's no doubt. They have the skill to back up that arrogance.

"I would love to," he says, cracking his knuckles, then stretching out his wings and tail.

"Do not go overboard," Thargar warns.

"Of course not. Besides, Khal is an excellent fighter," Typhon says.

I do not respond to any of the byplay between the two. They've been treating me like a golden child now and I am of mixed feelings about it. I have not changed since last week and the only thing that has changed is Tashak's approval. That does not sit well, but I cannot focus on that now.

Typhon and I enter the ring. He pulls his lochaber off his back and my stomach rolls. He intends this to be a more serious bout if we'll be using the traditional weapon of the Zmaj. Most battles are unarmed, such as mine with the lower warrior.

A dull ache forms in the back of my head as I reach for my own weapon. He leans his against his shoulder and gives me a quarter bow which I return, but my own is in full. Respect is earned and he has earned his. The familiar, simple motions stop all other thought and I'm in my center. My muscles alight, sparking with fire as my body prepares to fight, responding to the threat Typhon represents.

He moves faster than I can blink, swinging his lochaber in sweeping circles then slicing in from my left, not telegraphing his movement at all. I move fast, avoiding the blow, spinning around and slashing at his flowing robes, but he is not where my blade slices.

Whirling around, I barely dodge a kick.

I focus harder. This is no lower-level warrior. His speed and skill would tell me that even if I did not know.

His grin widens to almost a smile and he gives a slight nod of appreciation that I came so close to hitting him. We separate, putting a few feet between us, and each fall into a ready stance, facing off against each other.

"You're getting better," he taunts.

"Thank you," I say, remaining humble, knowing that he's trying to get into my thoughts, knock me off my center.

I will not play that game with him.

"So, you've seen the newcomers," he says. "What do you think, Khal? Any worthy mating material among these strangers? Rumors are flying."

He twirls his lochaber in front and around him with blinding speed. It whistles through the air making a music of its own, the music of battle.

"That is not a subject I feel free to discuss," I say stiffly.

My inner dragon roars defensively at his putting attention on Ashlee. She is mine. None may have her but me.

Something must show in my eyes that he picks up on. The grin is a wide smile and he chuckles before he moves. I don't see it coming. The butt of his lochaber catches me upside the head, knocking me to one side.

Pain explodes, blasting away thoughts and filling my head with stars.

Blinded I drop and roll, feeling his lochaber slicing

through the air where I was a moment ago. Rolling to one side I stop and leap to my feet, using my tail to rise higher, spreading my wings while swinging my lochaber quickly in front of me, making a defensive shield against any incoming attack.

Shaking my head, the stars clear slowly and my vision returns. But the anger is now pure, burning through, using doubts, fears, and frustration as its fuel.

Typhon rushes, pressing his advantage, but I'm ready. Ducking down and keeping my lochaber spinning, I catch the blade of his weapon with the shaft of my own, blocking his blow, but more importantly stopping him from pulling it back. A twist and thrust and he loses his grip, his weapon flying across the ring to land with a clatter.

His eyes widen and for the first time I see doubt in his eyes. He moves backward and I press the attack. Swinging, stabbing, and thrusting, forcing him to dodge each of my blows as he tries to work his way to his fallen weapon.

I don't let up. He threatened her subtly, but I don't care. She is mine. None may touch her. He may not even look at her with a hint of desire or I will cut it out of him and feed it to him while he bleeds out before me.

He ducks a blow then shoulder-rolls over to his weapon, picking it up as he rolls across it, but I'm on him before he can bring it to bear.

Swinging hard, with every intention of taking his head, I stop the instant my blade almost meets his neck. His wide eyes stare as we both pant, breathless.

"Yield," I huff.

Slowly, he nods. The sound of a dozen men gasping fills the arena. I take my blade away and store it on my back, offering my hand to Typhon. He takes it, rising.

We stare at each other. My hearts pound, breath coming in ragged gasps. Never have I performed so well. It's clear in his eyes he didn't consider the possibility I might beat him. I hadn't considered it possible either, until his subtle threat to Ashlee.

Everything changed in that instant. It wasn't a fight for me then, it was survival, protecting her.

"Good fight," he says.

"Thank you," I say, stepping back far enough to give him a full bow.

There is no point in antagonizing him or the others. The group of them stare, their gazes making my scales itch. Ashlee dominates my thoughts, images of her flitting through my mind, making it impossible for me to read the situation before me.

Are they angry? Will they respect me or target me? Doubts rise, but a messenger interrupts before anything else can happen. He races up, bows to Typhon, then to me.

"Tashak would like to meet with you," he says.

"Of course," I say, struggling to catch my breath.

Turning back to Typhon and the others I salute again.

"Thank you for the opportunity. My luck in this case is undeniable," I say, giving him a way to save face.

"Right," Typhon says, thoughtfully, one hand rubbing his neck where my blade was a few moments ago. "We'll talk."

There's nothing more to be said so I turn and follow the messenger. The fight replays in my mind's eye, focusing on the moment I felt like he threatened Ashlee. He didn't, not really, no Zmaj would. His words were intended to be playful, of that I have no doubt. My reaction was out of proportion to the threat they represented.

Because of her.

I love the Order. I truly do. It is all I have ever known, but for the first time I wonder what else there could be.

Ashlee represents another aspect of life, one that is completely new and exotic. She said one does not choose love, that it just is. That rings true for me and deepens my understanding of Archion's plight.

I saw it as a choice, an unwise one at that, but now...

We arrive outside Tashak's office door and I thank the messenger before walking in. Tashak is sitting behind his desk, clearly awaiting me.

"Thank you for meeting with me, Khal," he says, an unnecessary courtesy.

"Of course. How may I be of service to the Order?"

Tashak nods, folding his hands in front of his flat stomach, sitting straighter on his stool.

"Yes. It is on the subject of your brother. I know it is a topic that has been discussed and re-discussed. But I want your opinion on a very specific matter."

"What matter?" I ask carefully.

"Do you believe your brother should be demoted?" he asks, his eyes boring into me.

Demoted?

"No. I do not," I answer immediately and truthfully.

There's a brief flash of surprise on his face, then he nods slowly. His fingers, interlaced across his stomach, tighten and his eyes narrow.

"You do not think Archion should be demoted," he repeats, as if making sure he heard me correctly.

"Correct."

He raises a brow, leaning forward, seeming to find that very interesting. I knew the Order would not look upon his actions favorably, but I cannot agree with this line of questioning. It is unclear if Archion has lost favor creating an opening for my advancement or not, but it would be a mistake.

He is an excellent fighter, an excellent leader. Perhaps I can ask—

The loud gong of the alarm reverberates through the

office. Tashak leaps to his feet and races toward the door as I turn too. Both of us leave the office, Tashak going in one direction and I in the other.

I race through the tunnels to the upper levels, seeking the source of the alarm. Others race to their posts and we squeeze past each other. The sound of the gong continues, echoing off of the carved stone walls.

Emerging from the tunnel into the hallway that leads to where Archion and the females are being kept, I spot Nora walking unaccompanied ahead of me. I redirect my trajectory, wondering how she arrived here.

"Nora!" I call out as I close the distance between us.

She does not respond to my call. In fact, the closer I move toward her, the more I start to realize something is wrong. Her eyes are not focused, her expression is too smooth. She looks as if she is sleepwalking.

"Archion," she calls out, looking around. "Archion, where are you?"

A sea of soldiers of lower rank appear, racing down the tunnel toward us.

"No!" I order, turning to face them. "Leave her be!"

Tashak appears behind the group of them, confusing matters even more. His eyes go to Nora and widen in surprise. He pushes through the guards, stopping in front of Nora but not touching her. He crouches down so that his eyes are level with hers.

"A vision," he says.

Nora stops moving and mutters, looking at Tashak with eyes so bright they are almost glowing. She starts speaking words in a tongue she could not possibly know. She raises her hands toward Tashak's throat, reaching out.

The threatening gestures breaks the hold of the hesitating lower ranks and two of them push past Tashak, intercepting her reach and grabbing her arms.

As if by fates' hand, Archion emerges from a side tunnel in time to see this.

"No!" he roars.

Oh no. I sprint toward them, but I am too far.

He attacks the ring of warriors, his speed and strength coupled with his experience is too much for them. The guards throw themselves at him but they are throwing themselves into a blender of destruction. Broken bodies fly out of the whirlwind of his rage.

"Restrain him!" Tashak screams, his face white.

Five guards are on the ground, severely hurt, but no one is dead yet. If I don't stop him, they never will. Pushing past Tashak I block the next two guards from entering the fray, bodily blocking them.

"Archion!" I yell, ducking his fist then blocking the other as it swings for my head.

I hit his bicep with a knife hand, a move he himself taught me. His arm goes numb and it's enough to jerk him out of his rage. He glares at me for an instant before whirling around to Nora. He wraps her in his arms, closing his wings around her.

The guards climb to their feet, groaning in pain. They look at each other uncertainly, then me. Closing my eyes, I take a deep breath and sigh, knowing what must happen.

"Restrain him," I order. "Archion, please, go along. No harm will come to her."

He shoots daggers over his shoulder at me, and the fire in raging in his eyes is now only too familiar to me. Knowing what is happening inside of him, I see his struggle to control himself until at last he folds his wings and turns, offering his wrists for the shackles.

Tashak glares at Archion, me, then the guards. His mouth moves as if he's going to say more, but the situation is under control. He snaps his mouth shut, nods sharply, and crosses his arms over his chest.

Nora stands still, silent, but her eyes are still unfocused, staring at things I assume none of us can see. She can't have known those words. It is not possible. Something more is happening here.

I need to talk to Nora.

Now.

16

ASHLEE

I jerk awake, sitting up, my heart in my throat and a cold sweat over my body. Something's wrong. Eyes wide, brain foggy, I look around trying to find what startled me awake. A sound? A movement?

It's like I'm moving through molasses and can't think.

Nora.

She's walking to the door. Weird.

"Nora?" I ask. She doesn't turn around or respond to my voice. "Nora!"

I raise my voice but she ignores me, pulling the door open and walking out. What the hell? Climbing unsteadily to my feet it takes me a moment to get my balance. She's out the door before I can move. No one stops her. Where are the guards?

Rubbing my eyes to clear the sleep, I move to the now-closed door and throw it open, walking out. A massive arm appears and I run right into it, painfully smashing my breasts.

"Ow," I cry out, more in surprise than in pain.

The two Zmaj guards stare, impassive, waiting to see what I do.

"She's out there. I need to—"

They cut me off. The one with his arm across my chest places a hand on me and gently but firmly pushes me back into the room and shuts the door once more.

I stare at the closed door, completely at a loss. I have no idea what just happened. All I know is that it is really strange. Nora was asleep across from me, taking a nap after being worn out by all the stress. Now she walked right out the door and the guards didn't stop her. She just walked right through.

Staring at the door, I pace the small room back and forth making useless motions with my arms. Three trips across, then on the fourth I can't take it anymore and go to the door again, throwing it open.

The two guards silently glare, turning enough that their bulk blocks my exit.

"Nora is out there!" I yell at them, raising my fists in frustration. Nothing. They don't react in any discernible way. Not a fidget, not a blink, nothing. "Damn it, she's out there! I have to go to her!"

Nothing.

"Get Archion then! Tell him, or Khal—"

The distinct ringing of a gong echoing through the halls cuts me off. Now they react, if not the way I want. One of them shoves me back into the room and slams the door so hard it reverberates. There's a clicking sound and something sliding across. Stumbling backward I barely keep myself from falling onto the piles of pillows. Then I race back to the door but now it won't open.

The gong continues to sound and there's the furious sounds of activity and people rushing around outside the door. Then someone is yelling, apparently someone is berating the guards higher up than them.

"How could she escape? One small female!" the new voice yells.

I listen, but the voice turns more muffled, leaving me pacing around inside the small space, wishing I could be out there. What's going on? Why did they let Nora go but not me? I have no idea.

Heck, if we were under attack, I wouldn't know unless and until our attackers were literally at the door. How long are they going to keep me a prisoner in here? I'm starting to go more than a little stir-crazy. Running my fingers through my hair, I exhale heavily then drop my arms to my sides. This is not what I signed up for. This was supposed to be a diplomatic mission. I wasn't supposed to end up imprisoned.

Seconds crawl past and with each one's passing nothing happens. The gong has gone silent, with no sound outside the door. The anger and frustration fades away like a fire sputtering out only to be replaced by cold fear. They know Nora is free. They have her. Is she okay? Where is Archion?

I'm alone.

A pressure falls onto me as if I'm suddenly blasting into space at two g's. I've failed. Nora is lost, Archion is lost. I'm the only one left and I'm never going home.

Closing my eyes, I shake my head and then my entire body trying to push that idea out. It's not helping and I can't give in to despair. Getting a solid grip on my proverbial self I stop pacing and take a seat on the cushions facing the door. If I'm going to have to wait, then I'll wait.

It isn't much longer before I hear footsteps outside the door and it cracks open at last. I'm sure it's going to be Nora being towed back in by a couple of guards. It's the only scenario that makes sense. When the door opens up it takes me a minute to register that I know the large body blocking the light of the hall and it's not one of the guards.

It's Khal.

"Where is Nora?" I ask, not waiting to demand answers.

He closes the door behind himself, his eyes watchful.

"She is in good hands," he replies obliquely.

Bullshit.

"She needs to be brought back here immediately," I demand, shoving my finger down toward the ground. "I don't trust any of you with her alone."

"That is completely out of my hands," he replies.

"I don't believe you," I retort. "You've been in charge of us the whole time we've been here. Go get her back!"

He walks over, stopping right in front of me.

"I cannot!" he growls. "I am not in control!"

It's my turn to snarl with frustration while stepping back from his invasion of my personal space.

"What are you doing here?" I ask.

His mouth moves as he starts to answer but he pauses, closes his eyes for only an instant, then when he speaks his voice is calmer.

"I wanted to ask you if you know how Nora did what she did."

I shake my head.

"You and me both buddy," I mutter. "I have no idea what she did. One second she was sleeping, next she was walking straight toward the door." I throw my hands up in the air. "And the guards let her pass right through without any argument!"

"They let her pass?" he asks, an odd tone to his voice.

I nod.

"And when I tried to follow, they stopped me." I shake my head, frowning.

It's even weirder to recall it.

"I want Nora back," I demand once more, turning toward him.

When I turn his eyes are focused on me. Maybe I'm just imagining it, but it seems he's looking at me differently.

"Do you know what she did to escape the guards?" he asks.

That's not the only thing his eyes are saying. They're a little too warm, a fire burning in them that is calling to me despite all the chaos and confusion. I frown, trying to ignore my body's response to his fire.

"She didn't do anything so dramatic as escaping," I mutter. "She just walked out and they let her."

Is it getting hot in here?

"That cannot be correct," he says, frowning and shaking his head.

"I don't know what else to tell you," I respond, throwing my hands up in the air. "I've never seen anything like it before."

His frown deepens then he nods slowly.

"I see," he says, finally seeming to understand.

"At least somebody does," I mutter, shaking my head. "I have no idea what's going on."

I drop down onto one of the floor cushions, setting my head in my hands.

"Have dinner with me."

I raise my head, unsure that I heard him incorrectly.

"What?"

"Have dinner with me," he repeats, his eyes intense.

I shake my head.

"No."

That's all I say. It's all he deserves after acting like he did.

"Have dinner with me. Please."

I shake my head again.

"No. Why should I have dinner with you now after..." I trail off, embarrassed.

"I am sorry," he says gently. "Please. Share a meal with me."

His eyes are imploring, gentle, warm. I know this is about more than dinner. I stop myself from refusing again. Be practical not emotional. How else am I getting information here? Nobody else interacts with us.

Even the guards are just that, refusing to have a conversation with anybody. If I want to learn anything, this is the path forward. I need information, both on Nora and Archion, as well as on the Order itself.

At this point, saying that I'm distrustful of the Order is a massive understatement. I have no idea what their intention is, but I do know I don't like being held prisoner here. I'm at the point now that if I do make it back to Rosalind, I feel like I'm going to have to say we shouldn't ally ourselves with the Order. That we might even be enemies.

"Fine," I relent.

His face brightens.

"Thank you," he responds gravely. "I will go gather a meal."

He leaves quietly. I sigh, resting my head on the table. This is a cluster fuck. I don't know how we're going to fix this in any appreciable way, but I can't lose hope that we can.

By the time Khal comes back with the food, I've composed myself. He sets the food out on the table and settles onto the cushions across from me, then he serves me and then himself, the epitome of politeness.

I appreciate it, but what I want more is information. I wait until we're well into the meal before I ask anything important, talking about the food until the right time.

"Any news on what they're planning to do with Archion?" I ask.

His eyes darken and he shakes his head.

"All I know is that protocol is being followed," he responds cryptically.

I shake my head.

"What about Nora? What are they doing with her? Why haven't they returned her yet?"

"I am certain the protocols are being adhered to and she will not be harmed," he says, again avoiding the issue.

I stare as frustration slowly boils.

"How many people are here with the Order?" I ask, changing tactics something more general.

"I can't reveal any of that information," he says, meeting my eyes.

"Let me guess…it's part of the protocols."

"Yes," he smiles.

I huff, shaking my head and setting down my food.

"What are these protocols?"

His smile widens, but he doesn't respond.

Great.

Shaking my head, I reach out to ladle some more stew into my bowl, just as Khal attempts to intercept and do it for me. Our fingertips brush, the small touch sending a tingle of heat through me. I jerk back, my eyes going to his. The knowledge of the same heat is in his.

"Allow me," he says in a husky voice, ladling more food into my bowl.

I break eye contact. I can't meet the fire in his eyes any longer without doing something stupid.

"Thank you," I say, my voice tight.

I sip some of the slightly too-hot stew. That one light touch changes the dinner. Our conversation is stilted now, the anger and frustration shifting into something completely different. I catch his eyes lingering on my lips and then drifting down to the skin exposed by my slightly unbuttoned shirt.

His voice is husky as he steers the conversation to something less incendiary. While we talk about what kind of vegetables they have, all I'm thinking about is what he might look like naked.

Shit. I'm supposed to be keeping my head here!

I reach for a piece of cut fruit on another platter, but Khal stops me, placing his hand on mine. Tingles run up my arm, making my heart race.

"No, try this one," he says, picking up a juicy-looking wedge of yellow fruit.

He brings it up to my mouth rather than setting in my hand. I really shouldn't, but I open my lips. His eyes are glued to my mouth as I take a bite of the juicy fruit and sweetness bursts in my mouth. He pulls back the fruit and I lick my lips. His eyes darken.

"Good?" he asks, his eyes rising from my lips.

They're so hot at this point that I feel an urge to fan myself. I nod, not trusting my voice. Still holding my gaze, he pops the other half of the fruit into his mouth, chewing. Oh man. How do I defend against this? I can't even meet his eyes the rest of the meal. Luckily, it's winding down.

"One moment, please," he says, getting up and walking over to the door.

What is he doing? He opens it and talks to one of the guards, which leads to an odd whispered argument where I can't make the words out. I can't be hundred percent sure because they're far away and talking in low tones, but it doesn't sound like they're speaking the Zmaj language that I'm familiar with.

They have a different dialect? I'm sure if I ask, I'll be told that protocols stop him from replying. The argument ends and Khal beckons to me.

"Come with me."

"Come with you?" I repeat, and he nods.

"No, thank you."

"What?" His eyes widen in surprise and his mouth drops open.

One of the guards beside him smiles, but Khal looks at him and he quickly wipes the expression off his face.

"Why not?" he asks, turning back.

"Nora still hasn't come back. How do I know you'll bring me back here? That I won't be disappearing somewhere?"

He sighs, shaking his head.

"You have my word that I will be returning you safely," he says gravely.

I raise a brow.

"Your word?" I repeat.

He nods. What the hell? It isn't like he couldn't do whatever he wanted anyway. I'm not any more safe here than I would be anywhere else in this place. Besides, maybe I'll actually gather some intel once I'm out of the stupid room.

"Okay, fine."

"Thank you," he sighs.

He gestures for me to walk ahead of him. The guards give me hard looks as I step past them, but they don't try to stop me. That's a first.

I fall into step beside Khal, walking through a hall that looks like a variation of the room we were in, smooth-cut walls that can't possibly be natural, all a sandy-brown color with streaks of red. He doesn't lead me far and I don't really see much beyond the hallway.

"Through that door," he says, pointing ahead.

We go to the door and he produces something that looks like a key which he uses. The door clicks and he pushes it open. He steps to one side and indicates I should go through first.

I walk out onto a balcony that overlooks a small area outside that is covered with beautiful flowers. A cacophony of colors. Purples, blues, oranges, yellows, pinks, lavenders. It's stunning, especially here where everything so far has been drab and monotonous. It's so incongruous that it takes me more than a moment to process it all.

"Oh, wow," I whisper, stepping out further.

The gorgeous plants are growing in absolute defiance of the natural order of Tajss.

A refreshing drink for a parched soul in the clearly manicured and well-tended garden. It's a geometric design carved out with walkways and perfectly designed landscaping fit into a thirty-foot-square space.

It's perfectly symmetrical, an almost starburst design starting from the middle and expanding out, with smaller design pieces within. It's anchored by bushes and trees amongst the flowers, giving it an odd mix of manicured and natural that is truly arresting.

"How...?" I whisper reverently, afraid to spoil the beauty with the harsh sound of my voice.

"There is a small spring that spouts out of the ground almost directly in the center of the garden," Khal points out. "We use it to irrigate the area."

"Why isn't anybody down there?" I ask, seeing the pathways. "Or at least here looking down at the garden? I'd be here every day!"

He chuckles. "That hallway hasn't been used for some time. Neither has the garden, apart from it being maintained."

He points out across the garden and I look to where he's pointing.

"Do you see that pattern over there?" he asks, gesturing toward an odd star pattern I've noticed it in various motifs in the small parts of this place I've seen.

I lean over, squinting to see more clearly. When I turn my head to answer him, he sets his mouth against my own. It isn't any less mind-blowing than the first time. Stepping closer I curl my hands around his strong neck. The feel of him against me is intoxicating.

How can I not want this? How have we been staying away from this heat?

Khal breaks the kiss, pulling back, his eyes glittering with the same desire coursing through me.

"Let us return to the room," he says hoarsely.

"Yes," I agree, letting him tug me back through the doors.

He leads us back down the hall, past the guards and through the door. They give us odd looks, but I don't think much of it. I'm too focused on what I know is coming. As soon as the door closes behind us, Khal pulls me back into his arms and I sink back against him.

He feels so good, so strong against my own body. And his kisses...

I try to get closer. His hands slide down and cup my butt, raising me higher up against him so the kiss is easier to maintain. I sigh against him, my fingers sliding into the silk of his hair.

Yes. More.

Turning us around, he starts to walk so I wrap my legs around his waist, but I don't take note of where he's taking us. I'm fully focused on something else completely. The hard shaft pressing against the cloth covering my pussy consumes my attention. I know exactly where he's taken us when my back hits one of the pallets on the floor.

Horizontal? Yes, please. I tug at his robes then I break the kiss.

"Off," I huff hoarsely, pushing at the voluminous fabric. "Take it off."

He doesn't argue. Between one breath and the next, he's down to skin, covered in delicate scales, each one overlapping the one below it. The scales catch the light as he breathes, causing tiny rainbows to my eye. The edge of the scales are tinted with bright yellows and greens and seem somehow alive, expressing his burning desire. My hands itch to touch him, but he doesn't get back on top of me to make it easy.

His cock is massive compared to a human, and I've heard the stories—all the girls have—but seeing a Zmaj dick for the first time is breathtaking. Literally. It's not only the size, impressive as that is, but it's ribbed. Actually, god-honest ribbed for my pleasure. Yay me!

The underside looks soft, but the top has a bony rib structure going down to the base of his pelvis where I see a bone knob. It only takes me an instant to realize that protrusion is designed to hit my clit when he's fully inside of me. Hot damn, this is going to be good.

His eyes go to my own clothes and he arches an eyebrow. His cock bounces up and down, bobbing as if calling me to it with a summoning spell.

"Got it," I respond to his unvoiced question, sitting up to chuck the shirt over my head rather than dealing with the buttons.

I slide off my pants and underwear in another go and then I'm as naked as him. He stares at me, the look in his eyes making me clench my thighs together. It's almost too much, that look. Like he wants to... consume me.

"Come here," I urge, raising my hands to him.

His eyes meet my own as he complies, being sure to keep his weight off me with his forearms.

"You are the most beautiful thing I have ever seen," he murmurs, his eyes an inch away.

I've never believed anyone more. Reaching up, I pull him back into a kiss, pouring all of the desire I have for him into it. He returns it and then some.

Sliding my hands down his muscled back, my hands hit

the curves of that truly amazing butt. I have to squeeze it. He breaks the kiss, rising up above me. His eyes track down, stopping at the curves of my breasts. I watch as he raises a hand, cupping one of them gently, his gaze utterly fascinated.

"You are so soft," he murmurs, caressing lightly with his fingertips.

I make a sound when he inadvertently brushes over my already-hard nipple. He stills, noticing the small reaction. So he does it again, focusing his attention on the tight point. I squirm under him, closing my eyes so I don't have to see him watching me so closely.

I completely miss when he bends over to kiss me there. I jerk at the warmth of his mouth, sliding my hands over his broad shoulders. He nuzzles me, his breath hot against my sensitive skin. Then he scrapes his teeth gently over the sensitized flesh.

I cry out, arching up against him.

He stays there for...a long time. Kissing, licking, sucking. Nuzzling against the undersides where the skin is even more sensitive until I can't stay still underneath him, my skin breaking out in a light sweat, my legs slowly moving in response. When he lifts his head, he looks almost drunk.

His eyes are at half-mast, his cheeks flushed, lips swollen. Then he moves down.

I bite my lip as I watch him settle between my legs, his large hands pushing my thighs apart. His eyes don't stay on mine after that. His fingers trail across the embarrassingly wet flesh there.

"So soft," he mutters.

And then he leans in and licks a long line up my length with the flat of his tongue.

"Oh God!"

My hips try to raise up, but he holds them down. He's a quick study. He attacks me with his mouth, with his tongue, making a soft humming sound of enjoyment as he seeks out every nook and cranny.

Until he fully discovers my clitoris.

The reaction I have from that first light touch is enough to have him shifting all his focus there. I cry out, my hands digging into the pallet on either side of me when he seals his mouth just there.

And sucks.

That's it.

"Oh!"

I try to hold in my cries, but I'm not all that successful as the orgasm rips through me. Hot and deep and oh so necessary at that point. He keeps me up there, his mouth not stopping until I tug at his hair.

"Enough," I gasp, tugging him up. "I want you inside me."

His breath isn't exactly steady now either as he sits up and settles back onto his knees.

His hand curls around his length.

"You are small," he remarks, staring down at me.

"It'll fit." Hopefully. "Just... go slowly."

He shakes his head.

"I will hurt you. It is not a good idea."

Oh no. We're not getting this far and then turning around. Sitting up, I crawl over to where he's still on his knees and straddle his lap. His eyes scan me with a hunger that only stokes my own as his erection bumps against me. Close to where I want him, but not quite there.

"I'll control it," I tell him, kissing him lightly. "Okay?"

"I..."

He trails off, his hand clenching at my hips. I'm going to take that as a yes. I reach down and take him in my hand, aiming him up toward me as I rise up.

I take a deep breath as his blunt head hits my entrance. This is going to be tight...

I drop down slowly, one inch at a time, up and down to help him slide in. It is tight. Almost too tight, but I want him so much and I'm so wet from that first orgasm that I somehow make it work.

I slide down onto him until he is fully inside me. My eyes are clenched tightly shut, my breath coming in gasps once more. I'm beyond full. And I can feel his heartbeat deep inside.

Khal kisses my face, my neck, my shoulders, his hands touching every inch of skin he can as I adjust to the intrusion.

I collapse against him, leaning against his strength for a moment. Until I can't stay still anymore. Leaning back, I grip his shoulders, our eyes meeting as I slowly rise up and push back down.

His eyes cloud as the sensation hits him, his nostrils flaring, hands gripping my hips once more. We start to work together. I rise up, but his hands help me, steadying my hips, taking some of the weight. When I drop back down, his hips thrust up. And I feel exactly what all those ridges are for.

I cry out as my clitoris is stimulated exactly right. It's the hard turning point.

Soon, we're going at each other so fast, the sound of flesh slapping against flesh is loud in the small room. Sweat drips down my body, my face tucked in against Khal's shoulder now. The second orgasm hits me like a freight train.

I muffle my cry against his skin, my fingernails digging into his back as I shove myself down against him, grinding against that last ridge. Khal growls, shoving himself in that last inch and joining me over that glimmering edge.

I feel him jerk inside me, his body shaking as the sensations wash through him. Then we just sit there, clinging to each other. Supporting my back, Khal carefully lowers me onto the pallet, slipping out of me in the process.

I sigh, luxuriating in the softness as he comes down on top of me. My eyes snap open as I feel an erection nudging at me once more.

Second penis. The Zmaj have two!

I totally forgot that fact until this...oh.

Khal leans down to kiss me as he starts to thrust once more, this time slow and steady. Gentle and long, until the orgasm is kind of a gentle shimmer sliding through me. Khal comes quietly the second time too, his mouth still on my own, our breath mingling. I am completely done after that one.

I half feel Khal sliding in behind me and spooning me securely. I'm totally down for the count and I've never slept so easily.

17

KHAL

*S*he falls asleep lying on my chest. I watch her sleeping face, unable to take my eyes away. Her cheeks are flushed, her lips slightly parted, her hair just a bit mussed. I have never seen a lovelier sight. All I want to do is stay there in the pallet with her, hold her close, and drink in her presence.

But I should not be here at all. Should not have done what I just did. I ignored duty, ignored protocols completely and simply indulged in what I wanted. Reveled in the gift that is Ashlee.

Even though I know that what I did was wrong, I cannot regret it, but I should not stay any longer. I cannot fix what I have done, but maybe I can stop myself from falling further. Willing myself to move, but I don't. Ashlee is nestled in against my side, her head on my chest, her breathing causing her chest to rise and fall.

I know what I should do, but it is completely the opposite of what I want to do. I struggle with that reality for quite some time, lying here and staring at Ashlee's face. Wishing for a different reality. One where this would be simple, but that is something I cannot control.

Taking a deep breath, I let it out slowly as I pull my arm out from under her and lower her head off my chest to one of the soft pillows. She frowns slightly in her sleep, wrinkling her pert little nose, then she settles back down once more.

I sit up, eyes still locked on her. I do not want to leave, but I must. Duty is not convenient. Protocols are not convenient. If keeping them was easy, then we would not be who we are. I cannot lose sight of what I have vowed to uphold.

Even when it is not convenient for me. Even when it tears me apart inside. I stand up and look down at Ashlee, scanning her, attempting to memorize how she looks right then. I know I will never forget.

I dress quietly before I turn toward the door. Every step feels like I am ripping something away from my heart, but I continue.

I am not weak.

I take my obligations very seriously. I do not look back when I open the door, because I know, deep inside, the sight of Ashlee could break me. So I step outside and close the door behind myself.

The same guards are still at the door. They do not hide their disapproving looks. There is no chance that they do not know what just occurred in that room between Ashlee and me.

There is nothing I can say to defend myself, so I ignore the looks of disapproval. I feel enough of that emotion myself not to absorb everyone else's as well.

My first order of business is to find Archion. Luckily, that does not take long.

When I go to check in on Nora, I find him there, sitting beside the bed, holding her delicate hand in his own. I am glad Tashak allowed him to have access to her. She is sleeping soundly in the medical area, hooked up to various machines and being monitored by two Zmaj. The visual of the area is a bit intimidating, but Archion doesn't seem to notice anything but Nora.

My gaze falls to his large hand holding her much smaller one and, for the first time, I feel a part of me awaken inside. Absent one moment and completely awake and alert the next. The feeling is so strong that I stumble to a halt, overtaken by the swamping emotion. There is no question what it is. That part of me awakens along with a knowledge that I have a mate as well.

Ashlee is meant to be mine. She is mine.

It's a bittersweet realization.

The joy of knowing I have found my mate clashes with the pain of knowing it conflicts directly with my duty, directly with my obligations to the Order. I don't know what to do, but it's clear I cannot function with these emotions roiling inside of me.

I push it aside for later with great difficulty because right now I need to function. These emotions cannot paralyze me. My chest aches even when I try to set aside this new knowledge, this conflict inside me.

I step back, deciding not to interrupt Archion or the medics. I won't help him or them in the state I am right now. I need to be alone and find some control over myself. Turning away, I return to my quarters and lie down on my cold pallet.

Alone.

When I close my eyes, the empty space next to me is a throbbing ache, holding my attention. I imagine Ashlee lying next to me, warm, filling the space that I know is hers. Where she belongs, next to me. Mine.

My quarters, my pallet have always been a place for me to recharge and nothing more. This is the first time that

I've found either lacking. It's because she's not here with me.

I do not fall asleep quickly. Thoughts of what Ashlee and I shared haunt me. Pull me toward her. A sudden urge to go to her, to throw it all away hits me, but I know I should not return.

It's an effort of will but I stay in place and attempt to clear my head. It doesn't work, but eventually I fall asleep due to exhaustion more than anything else. The sleep is not a deep one. I toss and turn fitfully, my normally placid sleep cycle well and truly ruined.

A knock on my door stops my tossing and turning. Rising, exhaustion lying heavily on my muscles, I open the door, expecting the worst.

"Tashak wants you," the smaller Zmaj at the door says without preamble.

"Why?" I growl.

He steps back, his eyes widening and his hands coming up defensively. Control slams in as he composes himself and he salutes.

"I do not know," he says.

"Fine," I say, dismissing him.

"Second dining hall," he says, backing away.

"Got it," I bark.

He turns and races away. Rubbing my face to scrub away the dredges of my fitful sleep, I straighten my robes and head to the meeting place. When I enter the dining area there is a meal set out on a side table. The long, low black lacquer table has intricately carved legs, the designs of which match the comfortable floor cushions set out in neat rows on either side. The seats are made of supple leather, undyed so it is a natural tan color that matches the earth tones of the room. The pillars bordering the room frame the intricate, colorful tapestries hanging in each section. There are more tables, but they are unoccupied.

Except for one where Nora, Archion, and Ashlee are sitting. The sight of her halts me in my tracks. I did not expect to see her, though I do not know if I could have prepared myself even if I did.

The three of them continue talking while I pause to take in her beauty. Her silky hair, her soft skin, the lively light in her eyes as she gestures with delicate hands. I want to pull her into my arms, claim her as my own, but my desire is not the only thing to consider.

It clashes directly with my sense of duty once more, a pained tangle that I do not know how to endure. No matter how I feel, I must fulfill my duties. I force myself across the room and sit down across from Ashlee, careful not to be too close. I do not trust myself.

Ashlee looks at me briefly, but then looks away. I can't read her face or what she is thinking.

"I am glad to see you are well," I say to Nora.

"Thank you. I don't know what happened," she says, looking at Archion.

He covers her hand with his own, concern on his face.

"It is okay," he reassures her before turning his eyes to me.

"Do you know what this meeting is about?" he asks.

"I was only told that Tashak needed to meet with me," I shrug. "I did not know you would be here."

The other three exchange glances. Fortunately, we do not have to wait much longer before the sound of a gentle gong fills the room. Archion and I rise. Archion grips Nora's elbow and helps her stand, just as I reach across to tug Ashlee to her feet as well. She gives me an uncertain look but follows along.

We do not have time to explain what the gong means before the doors open and Tashak enters, resplendent in his colorful robes. Guards flank him on either side, six in total, their gazes sharp as they take in the room. I know if we make even one slight untoward move, they will be upon us.

Dressed in the red robes of a Councilor's personal guard, they take up practiced stances across the room, shifting to stand directly between each pillar. It is as much to separate themselves evenly as it is for aesthetic reasons. The Council is not above ceremony. Tradition.

Tashak pauses, meeting each of our gazes before he takes a seat at the head of the table, his robes elegantly pooling around him.

"You may be seated," he orders.

Archion and I give a slight bow, Nora and Ashlee take the cue and mimic us. We take our seats as quietly as he did.

"Eat. We need to speak, but do not allow the food to grow cold," he says, waving a hand over his plate.

Archion serves Nora and I serve Ashlee before serving myself. Her gaze locks with mine as I hand her a filled bowl. Something passes between our locked eyes, but I break the contact. This is not the time.

"Nora," Tashak begins once we have settled with our food. "I am curious to know if this episode was the first one of its kind? Have you experienced others?"

Nora looks at Archion before speaking.

"It is the first that I know of," she answers, her demeanor guarded.

"Do you have any recollection of what happened?" he asks.

"Yes," Nora says, barely above a whisper, her gaze growing distant. "But not as if I were fully there."

Tashak nods, his gaze sharp.

"Can any more of your people do the same?" he prods.

"Nothing like Nora just did," Ashlee interjects.

"Really?" he asks, tilting his head. "What exactly can your people do?"

"What Nora did was unique," Ashlee continues, clearly skirting the subject. "But I have heard of people who have received... feelings, or visions I guess you would say."

Tashak leans forward, clearly fascinated as he listens to Ashlee and Nora speak on various instances. If he is interested, the rest of the Council Seers will be too. Perhaps this inquiry is the first progress toward talks centering around an alliance and trade.

It also weighs in on Archion's side. It is clear that everything else Archion was pitching is not as important to Tashak as what Nora did and other similar experiences that their group has had. Interesting.

We continue eating in silence, waiting for what Tashak will do or say next. Toward the end of the meal, Tashak sits back, a thoughtful expression on his face. Archion catches my eye and I know what he's thinking. He sees an opening and he's going to press into it.

"Have you reached a decision about my ranking... and about Nora?" Archion asks carefully.

Tashak looks him over, his face still. There's a beat of silence, then two before he nods slowly.

"You may retain your position if you wish," Tashak offers. "And your mate Nora is welcome to live among us."

I keep firm control over my expression. The complete shift in viewpoint is shocking in itself but Archion decides to take this opportunity to ask for more.

"Would it be possible to travel back and forth to the city?" Archion asks. "My thanks for being so generous, but I ask for my mate."

Tashak nods.

"I will take the matter under advisement," he says, firmly enough to end more discussion on the subject.

Archion nods and gives his thanks.

"I will be recommending someone remain posted in the city. I think it would act as a good gesture on our part. An indication that we are open toward a possible alliance. And, hopefully, a unified and long-lasting peace."

I would never have predicted this meeting would go this well. It is more hopeful that I know any of us anticipated upon entering.

"For now, all of you have clearance to move around the lower hall."

I sit up straighter at that. They're being allowed to move around? This is my opportunity. I start planning the tour I want to take Nora and Ashlee on and I hope Ashlee will find it memorable. Maybe I can arrange to be alone with her again.

My prime cock stiffens and throbs the instant the thought occurs. Looking across the table at her there's an ache in my core. I know this has gone too far already. The path before us is going to be difficult even with the Council shifting their position. How far will I be able to push this?

Will they let me have my mate? Will I have to choose between desire, fate, and my duty?

Tashak rises and exits the room escorted by his guards, leaving the four of us alone. I imagine they are as stunned as I am as we all sit in silence for a long moment. Archion exhales heavily and shakes his head.

"That was... unexpected," he says.

"Right?" Ashlee asks, shaking her head.

Her brow furrows and I'm enraptured by the wrinkle that forms on her forehead, the way her nose pulls up, and her eyes shine with bright intelligence.

"So..." Nora says, looking around the room. "This is good, right?"

"Yes," Archion says, his voice filled with certainty, but he looks at me and I know he's as uncertain as I am as to what happened.

Something has changed, but what it is or what it means, only the passage of time will tell.

"Let's show the females around," I suggest, keeping my voice carefully schooled so as not to betray any of my own confusion.

18

ASHLEE

$\mathcal{W}$e rise and leave the dining area together. As we walk down the tunnel where apparently the lower warriors tend to congregate, we naturally split into two groups. Archion and Nora walk along in front of us, while Khal lingers behind with me.

"Would you like a drink?" he asks, smoldering eyes locked onto me.

Maybe he thinks it's the best introduction to the lower hall, or maybe he just thinks it's a good icebreaker.

"The brewery is modest, but the drink is good," he adds. "Also the atmosphere tends to be relaxed with a lot of the other warriors ending their shifts there."

I nod at him, smiling slightly. A bar. On Tajss. The novelty of it is enough to intrigue me.

"Sure. I could do with a drink."

Why not? He smiles and the tension leaves his shoulders and face. Obviously he's relieved at my acceptance. Did he think I would be angry or hostile? I'm not sure but he leads me off from Nora and Archion. I share one last look with her and she gives me a knowing smile before she's out of my sight.

Great, am I that obvious?

Khal leads us into a dimly lit area. Small tables dot the open space and a long bar, exactly like something that would have been on the ship, makes it obvious that this is the brewery. It's incredible. Uncanny—is the consumption of alcohol in dimly lit spaces really a universal language? The novelty of it makes me giggle causing Khal to glance over his shoulder at me. I hold up a hand, giggling harder when he looks.

"It's nothing," I say, trying to keep my voice down.

The other patrons are glancing at me, causing my cheeks to warm. Khal nods and takes me over to the bar area where there are various drinks and mixed elixirs.

I look around the room, taking in the new space. The room is simple enough, with intricately carved symbols upon the walls, simple low tables with tough cushions to withstand food and drink, tapestries on the walls, and skins on the floor. The colors are warm in here, oranges and reds intermixed with the more natural earth tones. It's clearly a place to come when one wants to relax, the design deliberately meant to comfort. Currently, there are more than a few warriors congregating in groups, sipping at their beverages. A few are clearly on their fourth or fifth, their eyes at half-mast as they almost slump over tables.

The ones who are more alert watch us curiously for a moment before turning back to their friends. The novelty of humans can't last forever, I guess.

"You may sit here," Khal says, gesturing toward one of the stools near the counter. "I will prepare a drink for you."

I slide onto the stool, one of the few in the room. Zmaj gravitate toward sitting on the floor with their tails and wings to deal with, but apparently preparing drinks is easier upon a high counter.

"What are you mixing?" I ask, curious as he pulls a tall, slick mug from under the counter.

"Frizzna," he says, finding a bottle and pouring it into the mug. "It is sweet and warm."

I watch Khal pour careful portions, using a slim mixing stick to stir the liquid together. It forms a unique burnt-orange color. When he sets it on the counter in front of me, I can't help but admire it.

"Oh!" I exclaim, pulling the drink closer. "It's so pretty!"

He smiles broadly, nodding and motioning with a hand for me to try it. The mug is surprisingly cool to the touch. Almost frosty, which I would have thought impossible on Tajss. It can only mean one thing. Tech. Some kind of refrigeration is the only explanation, but there is no technology apparent.

That must be the reason Tashak allowed Nora and me access only to the lower hall. I don't know what they have, but the medical device that snotty medic used on Nora would also indicate they have working advanced tech. Probably against their protocol to tell us, just like everything else.

I kind of understand. Information has to be guarded until we're considered safe.

"It is known for its color and its sweetness. Try it," he urges, while I sit cupping the cool mug in my hands and allowing my thoughts to run rampant.

I nod enthusiastically and lift the mug to my lips. When I take a sip, my eyes widen in reaction, then I take a bigger sip.

"Oh, this is delicious!" I look at the containers he drew from. "Is there fruit in here? And how much alcohol is in there? I feel like there is a trailing warm buzz sliding down to my belly."

It's good. Really good. I take another sip. Khal nods, clearly enjoying my reaction.

"A mixed fruit purée," he explains.

I nod, setting the mug down.

"This stuff could be dangerous," I observe. "I could see drinking two or three of these because it tastes so good."

"It has been known to happen," he admits, grinning.

I grin back and feel the edges between us softening.

"I appreciate the trust Tashak is showing for us," I say, leaning closer and keeping my voice down. "This tour is how I originally imagined the Order's outpost would greet us when we first arrived."

His expression turns serious. He leans against the counter, keeping his voice low as well.

"I know we have not treated you with the best of manners," he says. "There were a lot of suspicions for Tashak to dispel. It feels as though real progress is being made. Tashak is speaking with the Council now. We will know soon enough if they are interested in moving forward and planning a meeting with Visidion. Before Nora's episode... I was not at all certain that would happen."

I nod thoughtfully. After seeing what Nora is capable of, I had ascertained that they were leaning toward a yes, but I also haven't met the other Council members yet. Maybe they have even bigger sticks up their butts than Tashak does. What's even more interesting to me is the idea of appointing a diplomat to the city.

"So... Tashak mentioned the Council might appoint a diplomat to stay in the city," I say, looking up at him through my lashes. "It would be nice to have more time to... get to know one another."

The words hang heavy in the air filled with invitation and implication. Nice to get to know one another, yes. Nicer to wake up with him next to me.

But I can only imagine the conflict he's dealing with internally, and the fact that he has obligations and duties here. It's clearly affecting him. He leans against of the counter, his attention so focused on me that it's boring in with an intensity I've never experienced. As it has been ever since we left the meeting with Tashak. His attention is heady, and I don't want it to end. His eyes are warm as he regards me.

"More time with you sounds perfect," he whispers, a tinge of heat in his voice.

His eyes are dark, filled with thoughts that send a shiver down my spine. I clench my thighs together. He moves on to other topics, describing each of the spirits that are encased in the various bottles and barrels. It's clear the Order isn't against alcohol at least, but he could be talking to me about anything really.

He flirts with his eyes, with his focus, with his attentiveness. At the same time he remains deliciously mysterious. That's enough to have my heart opening a crack, enough to have me ready to follow where he leads.

"Would you like to see another chamber? One I opened specifically for us?"

His voice is low, his eyes hot, warming my skin as they drift up and down across me, scanning, drinking me in. It's clear what he means. Good thing I want exactly what he does.

"Yes," I respond simply.

He doesn't wait—grabbing my hand he leads me out of the brewery and down the hall, away from the prying eyes.

The chamber he leads me to is pretty. Plush rugs, one large tapestry on the opposite wall, but most importantly, there is a huge pallet with fresh white covers. Khal closes the door behind us and turns to me.

"I'm sorry I left you alone," he whispers.

I know he's referring to after...

"It's okay."

He shakes his head, stepping closer.

"I wanted to stay."

I nod.

"I know."

I do. I've been watching him struggle the whole time. He swallows, gingerly reaching out to touch my hips. When I don't move away, he pulls me in close, his eyes searching my own.

"I want..."

I don't wait for him to finish.

"Yes."

I raise my arms up, wrapping them around his neck. He sighs, leaning down to kiss me. This time it isn't the ravenous push toward completion, but rather a gentle coming together. I sink into the languorous meeting of mouths, my tongue slowly sliding against his.

We move over to the pallet together, in no rush as we sink into the plush cushion. We touch each other gently, the kisses long and deep. I sigh as his hand slides under my shirt, the heat of it against the small of my back sending a shiver through me.

The desire deepens and I start to feel that rush, that urge to reach the finish line.

Our hands grow impatient, tugging and pulling off clothes as we roll on the pallet, trying to get everything off without separating our mouths. We manage to do it, more or less.

When Khal rises above me, my shirt is still on but unbuttoned. Good enough. His eyes lock on my own as he sinks into me, his erection stretching me just as it did the day before.

I bend into it, wanting him inside me, my hands gripping his forearms tightly. I'm gasping by the time he's seated all the way, my neck arching back.

His hand slides down my front, rubbing at me as he starts

to move, his fingers dancing expertly over me. Remembering everything from before.

I orgasm, fast and hard, clenching down on him. He groans, stilling inside me, his fingers still moving. It flows through me, there and gone. Leaving me wanting more.

I relax again, my eyes opening slowly to see Khal staring with his jaw clenched. He's so hard inside me he feels like stone.

He doesn't move, holding himself rigid over me.

"I want you, Ashlee," he growls.

I swallow. Maybe it's an odd thing to say when he's buried hilt-deep inside me, but I know what he means. He wants me. Not just my body.

"I want you too," I return, searching his eyes.

His face softens slightly.

"Perhaps... we shall have each other," he says, starting to thrust once more.

Slow, gentle thrusts. I nod, not breaking that eye contact as I feel something unfurl in my chest. Something light and almost painful.

Hope.

That's what that is.

Hope.

I cling to Khal as he reaches his own end, hugging him close, just as I hug that feeling close. If only it can be as easy as it seems in this moment.

Hope.

It's all I can cling to as we build toward another climax.

19

KHAL

"What was your impression of Visidion?"

I watch Archion's face as Tashak asks the question. This private meeting with him is a necessary step. It would be irresponsible to continue any further without at least attempting to gain some insight into what the Zmaj leader of their group is like.

"He is... strong. Intelligent. Insightful." Archion tilts his head, clearly recalling his meetings with Visidion. "I was struck by his ability to see... into the person he is conversing with."

Tashak nods.

"I see. Is he a reasonable person? A good leader?"

"Yes," Archion agrees without hesitation. "He is a strong leader, one all the Zmaj and humans instinctively follow. His counterpart—his mate—is a human female, a leader in her own right. They have equal authority."

"Interesting," Tashak observes, interlacing his fingers over his stomach. "I imagine having representation for both the humans and the Zmaj is helpful."

Archion nods.

"I believe so. Between the two of them, they have the major perspectives in mind. They also like to hear opinions, other viewpoints. They are not inflexible in their views."

I hear a slight edge to that last statement that I do not think Tashak hears. It is clear Archion does not feel the same about Tashak and the Order, and he would be right not to.

As of late, I have also had my eyes opened to exactly how inflexible we are here and how that may not be the most intelligent or resilient way to be.

"Do you believe he will respect our ways, our boundaries if we move forward?" Tashak continues. "Or will he and his mate attempt to rule us as well?"

"That is a fair question. I do not think they have any interest in gaining another territory to rule," he admits. "They do not rule the mining settlement, but rather have mutually beneficial agreements with them. My understanding is that Visidion was the leader of the Tribe, and may still be, but he spends his time in the city, what we knew as Draconov. The Tribe is run by his former second-in-command, a Zmaj named Drosdan."

"That is good," I say, finally speaking up. "It would not go well for them if they attempted to take over the Order."

Tashak smiles thinly.

"Just so," he nods, as if coming to a decision. "The Council is leaning toward a meeting with Visidion," he discloses. "We might want a diplomat sent ahead for the first meeting." He leans toward Archion. "You have been to this city, have interacted with both Visidion and his mate. Do you believe sending someone ahead is a good idea?"

"I believe it is," I throw in, a bloom of hope starting in my chest.

"I agree as well. It is better to have another perspective. I believe it will put the Council more at ease before sending a larger contingent."

Tashak nods.

"With a diplomat in place to report to us, we will have more information and more time to discuss if forging ongoing ties will be in our best interest, as well as the best interest of the planetary community. A moon cycle or two without negative reports would likely be enough time to decide."

"That sounds like a reasonable—" I start, but my words are interrupted as a loud bang reverberates around us, loud enough that the ground shakes underneath our feet.

An explosion.

Tashak immediately shouts orders to the guards who burst in.

"Send regiments to scout out the trouble!" he shouts. "And rally the rest to ensure our stronghold is protected!"

The guards hurry to obey his orders as Archion, Tashak, and I race through the lower halls to the humans. I know Archion is thinking of Nora, just as my mind is fully on Ashlee and her safety. When we find them, however, I know immediately something is wrong.

"Nora?" Archion asks, slowing to a stop in front of her. "Are you... well?"

Her face is slack and her eyes are bright and shining. She looks as she did with her previous episode. Her eyes do not lock on her mate, but rather move to the Councilor.

Archion does not stop her when she approaches the other male, speaking in a strange, liquid language that I cannot understand, and it is clear nobody else does either.

Nobody but...

I frown, my attention shifting to Tashak. He is clearly listening to the message, apparently understanding the alien words. When Nora stops speaking, he turns to Archion with purpose.

"Go, join the fight," he orders.

Surprise crosses Archion's face, followed quickly by determination. It is a sign of newly restored confidence. He slams his fist into his palm and gives a half-bow in salute.

"Thank you for your trust. I will treat it with respect," Archion says.

"See that you do," Tashak responds with a nod.

I must go join the fight as well but I find myself turning to Ashlee first. Her eyes are already locked on me, filled with trepidation. I step toward her.

"I must go," I say, reaching for her hands.

She sets her own in mine, nodding.

"I know," she whispers. "Be careful."

"I shall endeavor to do everything in my power to return safely," I vow.

I cup her cheek, rubbing at its softness. She nods, raising her hand to cup my own.

"I know."

Not caring if anyone sees, I pull her into a tight hug, holding her close. I see Archion and Nora doing the same but we cannot stay here, as much as both of us clearly want to.

We rush out of the lower tunnels, completely in sync with one another. Almost as if all the dramatic events of the last few days never happened. There is nothing like a true crisis to bring everyone together, is there?

It does not take long to find the front lines of the fight. Luckily, the Invaders are not near the stronghold, our sentries having raised the alarms early.

They're not likely to even know where it is. Archion and I separate as we near the clashing groups.

Pulling out my lochaber, I get to work on the nearest Invaders, aiming for their exposed faces and throats. I have enough experience now to avoid the brown carapace-like armor all of them wear.

The shrieks are loud as the Order forces plow through

the Invaders, dodging their stunning weapons and their powerful blows. Their tusks are also stronger than they look, landing blows that can crack bone if one is not careful, but I am careful.

Flaring out my wings to gain lift, my arms raise and fall again and again, slicing throats, stabbing through eyes, bashing in skulls.

I feel no guilt or remorse. These beings have decided to attack Tajss and we are here to protect it. The math is simple. I fight alongside Archion for what must be hours, though time is an odd construct in the middle of battle.

All I know is to continue to attack. Continue to protect myself and my fellow warriors. This time there is another reason to fight, a deeper one that makes my blood burn hot.

Ashlee.

Nothing can threaten her and live. I will destroy the universe to save her if it was needed.

I do not look up, do not leave that battle haze until the second line of defense arrives to relieve us from duty. We have successfully defeated most of this group, but there are still others exploring the Order's territory and they must be stopped.

Archion and I return to the stronghold along with the other warriors we fought alongside, confident the reserve force can handle the rest.

"Good fight," he announces, slapping me on the back.

"Yes," I agree. "Good fight."

My mind is on Ashlee and I can see Archion's is already on Nora. We pause, our looks telling each other more than words ever could. He nods as we both decide to forego showers before we see the females.

The halls are eerily quiet after the resounding sounds of battle that we were engaged in. Two guards stand by their door, nodding as we approach. Archion leads the way, bursting through the door. I am right behind him. Inside Nora and Ashlee huddle together, leaping to their feet as we enter.

"Archion!" Nora cries out, running over.

Archion closes the distance and embraces her tightly, his eyes closed as she peppers his face with kisses.

Ashlee is not as vocal, but the relief in her eyes is clear when she pulls me into a tight hug.

"Come," I say in a low voice, picking her up and wrapping her legs around my waist. "Let us give Archion and Nora privacy."

Ashlee nods, ducking her head in close to my neck as I walk out with her in my arms, returning to the chamber I had opened for us before. Once alone, we do not exchange words. We say everything we need to with touch. Naked a moment after we are alone, we embrace each other on the pallet, the skin-to-skin contact necessary.

Raising her leg over my hip, I slide into Ashlee gently. She sighs, her eyes closing halfway as she accepts me. When she leans in to kiss me, I deepen it, my hands closing over her backside and her head.

I know the fight is ongoing outside but none of that matters. None of it is here, with her, where I want with all my heart to be. I have never had a better welcome back from battle.

20

ASHLEE

*W*hen I wake up the next morning, I see Khal and feel... happy. He smiles, leaning up on his elbow and kissing me lightly. My smile fades as I remember everything else. The battle that's still raging out there beyond the edges of the outpost.

The uncertainty about the future. Sure, Khal clearly feels something for me, but he's still a part of the Order and I worry the weight of all those protocols could be too much for him. He frowns.

"What is wrong?" he asks, sliding a soothing hand down my arm.

I lick my lips, covering his hand with my own.

"I... I want you to stay safe," I say, focusing on the most immediate issue.

Nothing else will matter if...

His eyes soften.

"Battle is a part of life on Tajss," he says, his voice gentle. "I am a skilled warrior and Archion will be there as well. We will watch out for each other."

I take a deep breath, letting it out slowly.

"I know. I just... Be careful."

No amount of assurances will get rid of this knot in my stomach, the tightness in my chest.

"I shall," he vows, his face serious. "I will come back to you, Ashlee."

I nod, turning into his chest, feeling too vulnerable with my face exposed and my heart on my sleeve. I'm not used to feeling this way, not used to the lack of control, if I'm honest.

We stay like that for a few more minutes, but it's borrowed time. We have to leave the pallet, leave the corner of this place where we are playing pretend it's just us. Our mood is somber as we clean up and pull our clothes back on.

Before opening the door, Khal tugs me in against him, hugging me tightly. I wrap my arms around him, leaning against his strength. Then time is officially up.

Khal turns to the door to open it but stops at a brisk knock. We turn to each other, confused. Who could it be?

Khal opens the door, revealing a robed Zmaj I don't recognize. He glances between Khal and me, but doesn't say anything, his neutral expression firmly in place. I appreciate that. Especially since my face feels like a furnace.

I step to the right a little to shield the bed and the rumpled covers on it that tell the tale of what went on in here, not that it isn't already obvious.

"Tashak asks that you and your... companion... please meet him near the first tunnel entrance."

Khal frowns deeply. I have no idea what the "first" tunnel is.

"The first tunnel?" he asks, as if he isn't sure he heard correctly.

The other Zmaj nods.

"Yes. Quickly, please," he adds, stepping back to make room.

Khal reaches behind him and takes my hand in his, gripping my hand tight, then pulling me closer to him.

"Thank you," he says, leading me away.

"What's the first tunnel?" I ask, trotting to keep up.

He notices and shortens his stride so it's easier.

"When this outpost was built, the original architects started with tunnels that branched out from the center, exiting far enough away that they would lead to safe points should we be under attack."

"Escape tunnels?" I ask and he nods.

"Essentially, yes."

Escape tunnels.

There would only be one reason for Tashak to want us to meet him there—he's expecting them to be used. But by whom? For what? Surely the battle isn't that bad...

We take a few winding turns then run into Nora and Archion before we reach our destination.

"Tashak summoned you?" Archion asks as they fall in step with us.

"Yes," Khal confirms. "Do you know what this meeting is about?"

"No," he says, his face and voice grim. "We will find out soon enough."

Well, he fits right in then with my and Khal's mood. I have no idea what to expect. Apart from anxiety, that is. I've been dealing with a consistent level of that since we got here, so nothing new really.

The tunnel entrance isn't much farther. I know we've reached it when Tashak's distinctive jewel-toned robes come into sight. He's standing in front of an already-open hatch with stairs leading down, three other Zmaj flanking him. I stare at the opening.

I'm pretty sure I've walked past this spot before and not

noticed there was a door in the floor. They did a good job camouflaging it.

"...tell them we must strike from the rear only after they pass the ravine. Otherwise they will have too much room in which to maneuver," Tashak dictates to another Zmaj, this one dressed in the standard sand-colored robes.

Tashak turns to us as the other Zmaj hurries away.

"We do not have much time," he greets all of us, his face tense. "We are currently adjusting our strategy to fight the Invaders. If we do not accomplish several counterstrikes quickly, the Invaders may very well travel close enough that they discover this Outpost. We cannot allow that to happen."

"Yes," Khal nods. "That can't be allowed, but Councilor— why did you want to meet here? Why are we not out there fighting?"

"The Council Seers were justifiably struck by Nora's abilities," he says, nodding at her. "Her ability to warn us indicates a prescience. One that is perhaps linked with Tajss itself."

"And?" Archion asks, eyeing the tunnel. "What does this mean?"

"It means we will entertain an alliance," Tashak says, gesturing to the open hatch. "Which also means you are free to leave."

Leave? Staring down at the open tunnel I rub my lips as my chest tightens and my stomach flutters. Going back to the city sounds great, but...

"Nora cannot go alone," Khal says, his expression still and voice deadpan.

He's voicing the same thoughts I'm having, though more diplomatically than I think I could say them right now. Tashak stares at Khal, his face a mask that might as well be carved of stone for all that it gives away. The two men match each other as seconds tick by, then Tashak smiles.

"Do you think so little of the Order that you serve?" Tashak asks at last. "Are we truly so monstrous? You and Archion will escort the females back to their homes."

"Thank you, Councilor," Khal says. His brow furrows and there is no doubt he has more he wants to say but he doesn't.

"No," Archion says.

No? What? My mouth falls open as I start to say something but no words come out. What does he mean no?

"No?" Tashak asks, calmly meeting the storm raging on Archion's face. The remaining two Zmaj guarding him stiffen but don't reach for their weapons... yet.

"Councilor," Archion says, his voice tight, his eyes hard. "Nora is my mate. I cannot leave her. I request..." He pauses, swallows, and at the same moment I see Khal's eyes widen. He reaches for his brother but Archion speaks before Khal moves. "I request I be exiled so that I may be with my mate."

"No." Khal's voice is barely a whisper, but it falls into the stunned silence and echoes off the close stone walls.

Tashak watches Archion closely, his head tilting thoughtfully to one side. His lips purse, his brow furrows, and the moments drag past as if time itself is fighting against moving, unwilling to see what comes next.

"Exile?" Tashak asks, also speaking quietly.

Archion seems to shake with pent-up energy or emotions too strong to contain. Khal is blinking rapidly, his mouth moving as if he wants to speak but can't. Archion swallows hard, then looks at Nora.

The war of emotions playing through his face and body stops. He's stock-still and the fire burning in his eyes is one of passion, love. Love so deep, so true, he's walking away from his life as it has been and fully embracing the one Nora represents.

"Yes," he says firmly.

Khal's eyes burn into me, drawing me to him, forcing me

to look away from the passion play that Archion and Nora are playing out. When I meet his eyes I'm burned by the intensity in them. The flames of his passion roar. My skin flushes hot and, embarrassingly, I'm wet and want nothing more than to jump on Khal and take him.

It's a physical reaction to something so much more than physical. His eyes consume me, burning past all my fronts, the parts of me I show the world, and looking at me naked, not physically but spiritually. Me. He sees me and accepts me as I am. Flaws, broken parts, whole parts, skills and failures. He accepts me as me and I see him too. He's throwing it all down, for me.

"Councilor," he says, his eyes not leaving mine. "I will join my brother in exile."

"Will you?" Tashak asks. "Both of you?"

"Yes, Councilor," the brothers answer in unison.

My hearts stops, breath stops, time stops as tears form in the corners of my eyes. Khal turns to face Tashak but his attention doesn't leave me for an instant. I'm wrapped in the warmth of his love.

Tashak rubs his chin, staring with a deep frown and furrowed brow. He looks at each of the men before him in turn, silent. My lungs burn, screaming for air, my muscles quiver, but he doesn't speak, and I don't dare to breathe.

"We are not monsters," Tashak says, sighing and shaking his head.

He doesn't say more, leaving us hanging. Waiting. What does he mean?

He looks at the two guards flanking him, neither of whom give any visible response. He raises his hands, then drops them to his sides. Khal's eyes dart to Archion. The tension is killing me.

"You are to serve as Ambassadors to Draconov," Tashak says, finally. "You are granted clearance to engage in general inquiries and basic resource disclosure, but that is it," he adds with a stern look.

Excitement races through me with a burst of hope and joy. Khal's eyes widen, my own shock and excitement mirrored in his expression.

"Thank you," Archion says, glancing at his brother then looking at Nora with a broad smile spreading across his face.

"Do not simply stand there—there is no time!" Tashak orders. "Go!"

"Thank you, Tashak," Khal offers, pulling me forward.

The Councilor nods.

"Perhaps we needed this disruption," he returns cryptically. "Now, go. Quickly."

He doesn't have to say it again. Archion leads Nora down the stairs and Khal follows, pulling me along behind him. I make it down four steps before the panic hits me and I freeze in place, unable to move.

Khal's strong arms wrap around me, pulling me tight. He leans down, his mouth close to my ear, his breath passing over my shoulder.

"I have you," he whispers. "Nothing can hurt you while I draw breath."

He holds me, not forcing me to move, doing nothing but holding me and strangely it's enough. His strength flows into me and in that moment, he becomes my rock. Forcing my eyes open, I stare into the swirling depths of his purple ones. Lips trembling I nod, unable to speak. He understands. Holding my hands he takes a step backward, down the steps. I follow him, one step at a time. The tunnel closes around us. Tightening and panic rises, but something burns in him, passing through the gentle touch of his hands on mine.

We continue, one step, then another. When we reach the bottom, the fear isn't gone, but it isn't controlling me. The trembling in my limbs stops and I take deep breath, exhaling slowly. I nod and Khal turns, still holding my hand, but the tunnel isn't wide enough for us to walk side by side. He leads the way.

My eyes adjust as we enter the tunnel itself, the length of it dimly lit with sporadic glowing rocks. It isn't short like that first tunnel we took was. This thing is long. Long enough to hopefully spit us out somewhere safe.

Archion and Nora are a ways ahead of us and Khal sets a fast clip leading us along. I rush to keep up with him. Time is definitely of the essence here, but the tunnel seems to go on forever, turning slightly at one point, but going mostly straight.

It's difficult to tell how long we've been down here for, but I would estimate maybe a full half hour before we see stairs leading up at the other end. By this point I'm out of breath and my thighs are screaming for a break, but we push through, climbing the steep stairs.

Khal and Archion lift the hatch at the top partway, popping their heads up enough to scan the area before disappearing from sight.

"Wait here," Khal says.

Nora and I nod, but nobody's there to see us. I listen intently, trying to figure out what's going on out there. I don't hear anything. Well, nothing until I hear that distinctive, familiar rumbling. Nora and I glance at each other.

"The rover," we say in unison.

Someone must have moved it here for us, for this purpose. Khal reappears, gesturing for us to follow.

"There are no Invaders in sight. We must leave while that is still the case," Archion says.

Copy that. Nora and I scramble up the stairs, blinking at the brighter light even though we're still in shade. This particular tunnel spit us out in a rift, which I can appreciate. Some cover is nice knowing the enemy is out there.

"Come!" Archion calls out, already in the rover.

We all hurry over, sliding inside. No sooner are the doors closed than the rover lurches forward, back out into the open desert. After spending so much time locked inside, it's almost a shock to see all this space. I reach out toward Khal without looking. He slips his hand into mine, squeezing it. I relax a little, my shoulders dropping as we gain distance.

All things considered... this turned out a hell of a lot better than I expected when I woke up this morning. I look over at Khal's profile, his eyes alert as they scan the area around us through the window.

Yeah.

I can work with this.

21

KHAL

I watch the desert around us, more aware of every danger that we could possibly encounter on Tajss than I ever have been, because of her. Everything is new, fresh, and different because she is in my life. My inner dragon has chosen. She is my mate, the one. She is more precious than my own life.

And for the first time, I feel a fear that I have not felt before as well. She is so vulnerable, so completely not suited to the harshness that is Tajss. I glance over to find her looking out the other window, her delicate profile beautiful, soft.

I will protect her with my life. There is no question.

Now, after everything that has happened, I marvel at how in control Archion was when he was separated from Nora.

"Khal."

I look ahead at Archion's warning tone.

"Yes?"

"Sismis, to the right."

Leaning closer to the window and looking up at the fast darkening sky, I try to spot what he's seeing. It does not take long to find the fluttering cloud of them flying directly toward us. Sharp teeth, talons, and leathery wings create a dark, foreboding mass. And then the screeching reaches us.

Blind, the creatures navigate through sound. Scavengers by nature, they are still a threat, able to tear and bite in a deadly swarm.

"What are we going to do?" Ashlee asks, craning her head to see the airborne threat.

"Do not worry," I reassure her, opening my door as Archion brings the rover to a stop. "Their ears are very sensitive." I hold up the whistle hanging from my neck for just such a danger. "This will be painful enough to drive them away."

"A whistle?" she asks dubiously.

"Yes," Archion confirms, opening his door and lifting his whistle up. He meets my gaze. "Ready?"

I nod and turn my attention to the sismis. I bring the instrument to my mouth, the smooth bone familiar and worn from time. Archion and I blow together. The sound is so high, we cannot detect it. When I glance at Ashlee, I see that she cannot either. It is out of range of the human hearing span as well. However, the flock of sismis reacts immediately.

The screeching increases, discordant as the cloud separates in confusion. They scatter individually, unable to navigate with sound any longer and attempting to escape the grating whistling, breaking their flock.

We don't stop the sound until they are out of sight, the stragglers dipping and weaving drunkenly. Only then do we climb back into the humans' rover and close our doors.

"Wow," Nora whispers.

"Yeah, that was... really easy," Ashlee agrees. "Where can we land a couple of those whistles?"

Archion and I laugh at that as he starts the rover and we move forward once more.

"I can make some for both of you," I tell her.

"Yes," Archion agrees. "But for now, we need to stop for the night." He scans the fast-darkening landscape around us. "It is too dangerous to continue our journey through the night."

"There is a small cave system over that rise ahead," I point out. "We can take shelter there."

Archion nods and turns the rover toward the indicated direction. The cave system is exactly where I remember it. It has multiple small caves that dot the rock formation, many of them connected to each other, with some stand-alone crevices.

We find two near each other and stop the rover right outside, partially blocking the entrance to keep out any of the larger predators.

"Stay in the rover," Archion orders. "Khal and I will hunt for dinner."

"Be careful," Ashlee implores when I turn to leave.

I turn back and kiss her softly.

"Yes."

Archion and I move swiftly, in silent accord. Neither of us wants to leave them alone for long, even with the protection of the vehicle. Moving into one of the interconnected caves, we separate, moving quietly. It would be very easy to scare skittish prey away in these echoing chambers...

I sense movement. Turning and swinging with my lochaber before I fully register it, I stab a small, furry round creature. A gretba, one of the cave-dwelling creatures of Tajss.

I lean down to pick it up, judging how much meat is on its bones. Enough for three. Carrying it back to the front of the cave, Archion is returning too, carrying a gretba only slightly smaller than my own. He eyes the one in my hand and grunts.

"Enough," he says.

"Yes," I agree.

Nora and Ashlee exit the rover as soon as they see us and look at what we caught.

"Oh... those are unfortunately cute," Nora remarks.

Ashlee nods.

"Sure, but we're hungry and they aren't going to waste," I say.

The females' eyes widen almost as one and they purse their lips. Ashlee shrugs but Nora pales at the prospect, hands moving to cover her stomach.

"I think I'm going to be sick," she gasps, then runs out of the cavern. An instant later there is the sound. Perhaps we should have skinned and dressed them before bringing them back, but what is done is done.

Ashlee and Nora get pallets out of the rover while Archion gathers kindling. He forms the material into a small pyramid shape then leans close and belches a small burst of flame to start a fire to cook the meat. While he works I skin and dress the gretbas. Ashlee brings out some metal skewers they have in the rover and I use some rocks to set the meat far enough away from the flame to cook evenly.

The smell of cooking meat and the glow of the flame is lovely after the darkness outside. Cleaning off my hands, I settle onto the pallet next to Ashlee to wait for it to cook. Archion does the same with Nora.

Ashlee smiles, cuddling into my side with a sigh. Holding her close, I feel... contentment. A warm blanket of comfort. I have not told Ashlee what I am sure of in my heart. I want to share the rest of my days with this beguiling female. Defending her, fulfilling every one of her needs, and simply basking in her presence, in a love so pure it managed to thaw even my heart, to break it free of the hard cage of duty and obligation.

That same heart that always felt separate, asleep perhaps, now feels vital and filled with light. She has changed me. Changed me in a way I did not even know was possible and for which I will be forever grateful.

I kiss her silky head, thinking of the endless days that were my life before her, one blending into the next. I have been renewed, given a new purpose. One that fills me up, warms me from the inside.

When the meat is cooked and I offer her the fruit of my labor, I enjoy watching her eat knowing that I was able to provide what she needed. When we lie down on the pallet together I cover her back with my own body, keeping myself between her and the mouth of the cave. There is a bone-deep satisfaction in keeping her safe.

I hold her close, knowing she is the most precious thing to ever come into my life and that I want her with me forever.

"Khal?" she murmurs, sleep edging her voice.

"Hmm?"

"I hope... you like... the city."

I tighten my grip. "If you are there, I know I will like it."

No response. When I look down, it's to find she has fallen asleep. I smile, lying down once more. I fall asleep some time later, but I do not allow myself to go to deep sleep. I must be able to detect any threat before it reaches us. When I wake up the next morning, it is with a smile upon my face.

"Morning." Ashlee greets me with a husky voice, her eyes warm.

I kiss that lovely smile and know this is how I want to wake up for the rest of my life. Next to Ashlee.

However, we do not have time to linger in the cave, not now. Eating and packing quickly, we return to the rover and continue on our way just as the suns begin to climb in the sky. We do not have much farther to travel and it is not difficult to notice when we are near.

The city is difficult to miss—the activated dome sparkling on the horizon long before it comes into view. When I first see the dome and the shadowy outlines of the structures it protects, I feel old memories stirring. There are faded memories of this place glimmering in the back of my mind.

The Devastation took so much. Recollection of what we once had is not even the greatest casualty. My memory of this city clashes with its current state. It is still grand, and obviously they found a way to power the shielding dome, but as we draw closer, I can also see the effects of time passing. The destruction wrought simply by the lack of inhabitants, but over that destruction, I also see a renewed hope.

As the rover pulls up outside the dome it's easy to spot recent repairs and some that are in progress. We step out of the vehicle and growing hope takes root inside me as I take in the city. Beyond the dome there are people, both human and Zmaj, walking around. Living.

This... this is a new beginning.

Possibilities play out before me, futures of what could be as our two races work together, bringing not a return of what was but creating an entirely new future. On the far side of the dome there is a group walking toward us with purpose.

It's made up of three Zmaj and one human female who strides a step ahead of the two males. She is dressed in pristine white with a flowing cape. Sharp features but sharper eyes that miss nothing. The three males with her carry an air of arrogance about them. One of them is slightly larger than the other two, but neither of them give away anything with their looks.

Nora operates the controls of the airlock and our group

files in, waiting for the process to cycle us into the dome and the city proper. When we exit the other side the female stands waiting, flanked by the males.

"Nora, Ashlee, Archion, I'm glad you made it back safely," the female says, her tone commanding, eyes steady on me. "And who is our guest?"

"This is Khal, my brother," Archion says, introducing me. "He has come as an ambassador from the Order. Khal, this is Rosalind, the Lady General."

I meet her steely eyes and see the bright, shining intelligence in them. I place my fist against my open palm and bow one quarter from my waist, not taking my eyes off of hers.

"It is an honor to meet you," I say.

"The honor is mine," she returns, smiling quietly. "I am glad the Order is considering forging ties with us."

"Yes," I agree. "I hope we can have a fruitful relationship."

"On that we can agree." She turns to the commanding Zmaj beside her. "This is my mate, Visidion."

"I hope you had a safe journey," Visidion comments, clasping my forearm in a warrior's greeting. His gaze is as all-knowing as I was warned it would be. His eyes are assessing me—my character, my intentions, and my skill. I have nothing to hide.

"Yes, there was no trouble," I say.

"Good." He turns to the others with them. "This is Ladon and Sverre."

I greet the other Zmaj, struck by the welcome from them. In my experience meeting any Zmaj is a gamble if they're not of the Order. Almost all of them I've met prior have been gripped by the bijass and our meetings did not end so well. I also observe the striking contrast to how the Order greeted Nora and Ashlee. I much prefer this reception.

"Come on, I'm sure you're all hungry after that trip,"

Rosalind interrupts. "Let's eat so you can then rest in your quarters."

"My thanks," I murmur, following the group through the city.

The signs of decay are more evident up close than they were from a distance but so are the efforts to repair and rebuild. Looking everywhere I try to take it all in at once. Broken glass, twisted steel, sand drifts, and debris dot the city blocks, but it's clear that this is being cleared away. They are productive if nothing else.

When we reach the town square foggy memories of before rise from the mists that engulf most of my thoughts. The massive statue that dominates the center fountain stimulates them. The statue that commemorated the rebellion.

Erected in honor. If only we knew then that it would also be our end.

Why... I don't know. The memory is gone as fast as it was there and I'm left only with an empty ache, a hole in my thoughts. A bittersweet sensation.

"You okay?" Ashlee asks, jerking me out of my reverie.

The others are staring at me, waiting. Shaking my head to clear it, I focus on her.

"Yes," I say, finally. "Sorry. An old memory."

"I'd love to hear it," Rosalind says.

"I'm sorry, it came and went in a flash," I say.

She nods, boring into me with those steely eyes that miss nothing. She weighs my words carefully before turning and leading the way into the building that sits directly behind the fountain. As I recall it was once the city offices.

She leads us through the open lobby and the sound of dishes clattering and soft voices fill the space. Female voices. We enter a room with multiple long tables, one of them set with food already. There are many other females here. Females and... children.

I stop in my tracks, staring at the babies and even older children. The happy sound of children giggling and playing strikes me in the chest. An ache so deep and hard hits me that I wonder if my hearts are going to burst.

Children.

Zmaj children.

Impossible. There are no females….

I look around, trying to spot a Zmaj female, but there are only the human females. One of the children races up to our group. It's a male, wearing loose flowing pants like the other Zmaj here. His coloring is brilliantly bright shades of yellow and blue. He skids to a stop in front of us, looking up at me.

"Who are you?" he asks, defiantly thrusting his chin out, a stick held aggressively in his hand.

"This is a friend Illadon," Rosalind says.

"Friend?" he asks, eyeing me carefully, not lowering his weapon.

Kneeling to be closer to eye-level with him, I nod.

"Illadon?" I ask.

"Yes," he says, chest swelling with pride. "This is my territory. Are you a friend, coming in good faith?"

"I am," I say gravely.

A smile bursts across his face like the suns emerging from behind the darkest of clouds.

"Cool!" he exclaims. "I'd hate to have to kill you."

He lowers his stick-weapon and holds out a hand. I take it, grasping it in a warrior's shake. He turns and runs off but I remain there, kneeling, staring after him as he rejoins another child. A female one. A warm hand touches my shoulder, breaking me from my reverie. I don't have to look to recognize Ashlee's touch.

This… this is why we must forge an alliance. This is a true future, a true reason to hope.

The children play, chasing each other and laughing as

they play games together. The females who were setting out food come over to our group.

"Calista, Jolie, this is Khal. He is Archion's brother and from the Order," she says. "He is here to serve as an Ambassador between our peoples."

"It's so nice to meet you, Khal," Calista greets me.

"Yeah, and I can totally see the family resemblance," Jolie adds, looking between Archion and me.

"It is a pleasure to meet you as well," I return, inclining my head to them both.

My attention keeps straying to the small children running around, both of them with sticks in hand, play fighting.

"Oh, that's Illadon and Rverre. They're four now and they never seem to stop competing with each other. Hey guys—stop it right now!" Calista shouts at the children.

I stifle a grin as one of the females climbs on the table and the male tries his best to swipe her legs out from under her. I can remember being that age, the instinct to compete paramount.

"Come on, let's eat," Ashlee urges, tugging me to a seat.

I follow her, feeling overwhelmed as I take a bite of the food.

"Oh, this is delicious," I remark, taking another bite to taste the sauce once more.

"Sure is. Too bad the chef won't share her recipe," Calista says, taking a bite. "Maybe if I sold her my firstborn."

The table laughs at the joke. I watch the interaction. Seeing the casual way in which Rosalind and Visidion join in. Rosalind has a kind of quiet, determined strength that emanates from her even now. She has no reason or desire to show she is in charge. It is clear and Visidion is an excellent partner to her.

I am struck at the difference between the Order and the

society they are building here. Hierarchy is of the utmost importance for us. But this... this feels...

Like a family. A home. People who care about each other.

I feel out of place and welcome at the same time. Ashlee covers my hand with her own and I know I could get used to this, quickly.

"Tired?" she asks.

I shake my head, turning my hand to squeeze hers.

"No," I murmur. "But I would like to be alone with you after you are done eating."

A light sparks in her eyes.

"Sounds like a plan," she says huskily.

The heat rises in me as we share small touches. Small, knowing glances. When the meal is done, we stand up as one. Visidion scans us, humor in his eyes.

"It seems as though you will not be needing separate quarters, Khal," he says quietly, in a voice only we can hear.

"I would like to remain with my mate," I say, nodding.

Ashlee goes still next to me, but she does not say anything. I turn with her, leading her out of the room.

"Mate?" she repeats once we are outside, alone.

"Yes," I say confidently, raising her hand to kiss it. "Mate. I have known since the beginning, I think," I add. "I was a fool to even attempt to fight it."

She smiles, her heart in her eyes.

"Yes," she agrees, startling a chuckle out of me. "You were a fool to do that." Then she turns away, tugging at my hand. "Come on—I want to be alone."

Since that is exactly what I desire as well, I hurry after her. Luckily, her quarters are not too far. Leading me to a nearby building, we climb up and walk down a hallway where she opens a door. Tugging me inside, she closes it, and we are alone.

Finally.

Picking her up, I walk her over to the large bed inside. She giggles when I toss her gently onto the pallet, the sound bringing a warm joy. I want to hear that happy sound forever. I take my time undressing her. Kissing every inch of skin I reveal as I pull off her shirt, then her pants, then her underwear.

Until she is panting underneath me, the tips of her breasts hard with arousal, that soft place between her legs wet and ready.

"I want a taste," I mutter, pushing her silky thighs apart.

"Khal..." she sighs, arching up to meet my mouth.

Mmmm.

I lick and suck at her, unable to get enough of her taste, of the delicious cries she releases when she's pleasured.

With one last lick, I rise above her, taking in her flushed skin, half-closed eyes, and slightly parted lips.

"Beautiful," I say hoarsely, sliding into her gently.

Her eyes flutter shut as I slide in, the feel of her encompassing me almost sending me over that fine edge.

"Ashlee."

She opens her eyes.

"You are mine, Ashlee."

I push in that last inch, carefully grinding against that sensitive nub. She cries out, her small nails digging into my forearms. Shaking her head, she opens her eyes to meet my own.

"Fine," she agrees, panting. "But you're also mine."

I smile, leaning down to kiss her deeply. When I raise my head, her breath is coming even faster.

"I was yours from the first time I saw you."

Her face softens and then suffuses with pleasure as I thrust in. I pour everything into the physical act. Everything I feel for her. The eternal gratitude I will always have that I failed to resist her.

I give her all of me.

When she cries, I cannot hold myself back anymore. The incandescent pleasure envelops me.

"I love you, Ashlee."

She wraps her arms around me, tugging me down on top of her until all I can see are her eyes.

"I love you, Khal."

I do more than I ever even thought I could. More than I even had the capacity to dream for.

I kiss her soft lips gently. I will cherish Ashlee forever and never forget the precious treasure I have been given.

THE END

ABOUT THE AUTHOR

USA Today Bestselling Author of fantasy and scifi romance, Miranda Martin's books feature larger than life heroes with out-of-this-world anatomy and smart heroines destined to save the world. As a little girl she would sneak off with her nose in a book, dreaming of magical realms. Today she brings those fantasies to life and adores every fan who chooses to live in them for a while.

She was born and raised in southern Virginia, but as a veteran she's traveled to places like Korea, Hawaii and good 'ole Texas. Now she's settled in Kansas, the heart of America, with her husband and daughters. Her favorite animals are dragons, unicorns and cats. If she's not writing, you can still find her tucked away somewhere with a warm blanket and her nose in a book.

Get in touch!
mirandamartinromance.com
miranda@mirandamartinromance.com

ALSO BY MIRANDA MARTIN

USA TODAY BESTSELLING AUTHOR

Red Planet Dragon's of Tajss Series
Red Planet Jungle Series
The Power of Twelve Series
The Alva Series
Dragon's & Phoenixes Series